GIANT
TALES

RETOLD BY FIONA WATERS

ILLUSTRATED BY AMANDA HALL

CHRYSALIS CHILDREN'S BOOKS

For Rob, of course, with much love – FW

For RW – AH

First published in the United Kingdom in 2004
by Chrysalis Children's Books,
an imprint of Chrysalis Children's Books Group plc
The Chrysalis Building
Bramley Road
London W10 6SP
www.chrysalisbooks.co.uk
This edition distributed by Publishers Group West

Retelling © Fiona Waters 2004
Illustrations © Amanda Hall 2004
Design and layout © Chrysalis Children's Books 2004

The moral right of the author and illustrator
has been asserted

Designed by Sarah Goodwin

A CIP catalogue record for this book is available
from the British Library.

ISBN 1 84458 143 8

Set in Walbaum MT and Bodoni
Printed in Thailand

2 4 6 8 10 9 7 5 3 1

This book can be ordered direct from the publisher. Please contact
the Marketing Department. But try your bookshop first.

Contents

Mighty Mountain

Many moons ago in ancient Japan, a baby boy was born in a remote village. A new baby was always a time for rejoicing but this baby was the object of even more interest than usual for he was huge. Not just big, but huge. His father was very proud of his latest offspring, but his mother looked upon him with some trepidation. How on earth would they keep him clothed and, more to the point, how much would he eat?

The answer was a very great deal, and the baby just kept on growing and growing so that by the time he went to school he was head and (very big) shoulders above all the other boys. But he was a gentle boy, kind to his mother—who was worn out with all the cooking she had to do for her huge son, never mind the rest of the family—and he was always ready to help his father in the fields after his lessons. He studied hard at school, especially history, and everyone loved him. He learned to wrestle and soon gained the nickname Mighty Mountain. And still he grew ever taller.

The years passed and Mighty Mountain decided it was time he sought his fortune outside his village. He had heard the emperor held a wrestling competition every year, and Mighty Mountain decided he wanted to win the competition. So he set off to walk to the capital where the emperor lived in a palace of many pavilions and gardens filled with rustling bamboo thickets. It was a long way, but the sun was warm on his back and, it must be admitted, Mighty Mountain was full of some very conceited thoughts about what he would do once he had won the competition.

As he walked alongside a clear rushing river, Mighty Mountain saw a girl filling two great wooden buckets with water. Her shining black hair was piled high and decorated with silver butterflies, her kimono was of the palest jade green and her feet were like tiny white mice peeping out from her sandals. She looked far too tiny and delicate to carry such a heavy load, so Mighty Mountain thought it was only right that he should offer to help her. He also noticed that she was very pretty.

"Let me carry that for you," called Mighty Mountain.

But as he scrambled down the riverbank to help her, she hefted the two buckets onto a wooden yoke and tripped daintily up the riverbank as though she were merely carrying an empty birdcage. And what's more, she was looking at Mighty Mountain and giggling.

He bent forward to take the yoke off her shoulders, but she snatched up his hand in hers and he realized that she was surprisingly strong. He went to pull his hand away and found he couldn't. He tugged harder, but still her grip remained firm, and in fact she was pulling him along as she walked.

Mighty Mountain grew rather red in the face as he struggled to release his huge hand from her tiny one. "Let me go, let me go!" he shouted. "I am on my way to the Emperor's Wrestling Match and I still have a long way to go."

The girl looked at him quizzically, her head to one side. "You certainly do," she said. "A very long way to go. I think you'd better come with me and meet my grandma."

Mighty Mountain was much too polite to say he didn't especially want to meet her grandma, and anyway she had still not released his hand so he didn't really have too many options.

"I shall carry you, if you like," said the girl as Mighty Mountain stumbled over his feet.

"Certainly not!" spluttered a furious Mighty Mountain. "I am Mighty Mountain, a great and fearless wrestler, and I am on my way to win the Emperor's Wrestling Match."

The girl looked at him closely. "I am sure you are a fearless wrestler, but I really think you should meet my grandma. She was thinking about taking part in the Emperor's Wrestling Match herself."

Mighty Mountain could not believe his ears.

"She would be very happy to help you achieve your ambition," continued the girl. "You obviously need to do some serious training," and she pulled Mighty Mountain along the path

with seemingly no effort at all, and remember, she was still carrying the two great wooden buckets as well.

Mighty Mountain had never felt so ashamed in all his life. Dragged along by a girl, like a great useless lump, his dreams of winning the Emperor's Wrestling Match seemed rather foolish now!

The girl led him up a steep mountain track towards a little thatched hut. As they drew closer, a woman appeared round the corner of the hut—carrying a cow in her arms! Mighty Mountain rubbed his eyes in astonishment.

"Hello, Mother," said the girl. "This young man wants to win the Emperor's Wrestling Match, so I thought Grandma might be able to help him."

The woman put the cow down carefully and looked at Mighty Mountain. "You look delicate, young man. I can see you need feeding up. I am delighted my daughter has brought you home. Grandma will be here shortly, she is just coming." Mighty Mountain bowed very low, rendered speechless by her cow-carrying.

"Oh, drat!" said a quavery old voice. An ancient and very tiny lady had just walked into the tree that stood outside the hut. "I do wish that tree wasn't there, my eyes are not what they used to be," she muttered. "In fact, that is the very last time I am going to bump into it," and so saying, the ancient and very tiny lady bent down and, wrapping her skinny arms around the trunk, she pulled the tree up out of the ground as effortlessly as if it had been a carrot. She threw it up in the air and away it whirled on the wind like a feather.

There was a loud thump, and Mighty Mountain lay stretched out on the ground. He had fainted clean away.

Kuniko (for that was the girl's name) looked at her mother and grandma and laughed. "You see? We have a lot of work to do if we are going to get him ready for the Emperor's Wrestling Match!"

So it was that the training of Mighty Mountain began. Every morning, while it was still dark, Grandma would haul him out of bed and throw him into the bitterly cold river. Up he would come, spluttering through the ice, and as he swam to the shore Grandma would throw a tree downstream which Mighty Mountain then had to pull up out of the fast-flowing freezing river.

During the day Mother made Mighty Mountain carry the cow from the barn up to the pastures and then back again as dusk fell. In the evening he had to practice wrestling with Grandma. He was afraid of hurting her, but it was usually the other way around.

Mighty Mountain did indeed grow mighty, and finally one day he managed to pin Grandma to the ground long enough to claim a win. Kuniko clapped her hands in delight, and Mother gave him such a thump on the back that he nearly fell over—nearly, but not quite.

"Hah!" said Grandma. "Now we have a champion who will win the Emperor's Wrestling Match!"

"If I do manage to win," said Mighty Mountain modestly, "I should like to buy you another cow."

Kuniko giggled, "We couldn't possibly accept such a gift from someone who isn't family."

Mighty Mountain smiled broadly and stumped up to Grandma and Mother, and asked if he could marry Kuniko! "Then I would be part of the family," he laughed, "and it would be quite in order for me to give you a cow, Kuniko."

Grandma and Mother were delighted and readily gave their permission. So that was all settled.

The next morning, Mighty Mountain did not wait to be thrown into the icy river, but set off for the Emperor's Wrestling Match. He walked through wind and hail and over thick snow, but he hardly noticed as he thought of how happy he would be once he had married Kuniko.

When he reached the emperor's palace of many pavilions and gardens filled with rustling bamboo thickets, he found many wrestlers there already. But they all looked flabby and fat, just sitting about, eating huge plates of rice. Mighty Mountain tied his hair up in an elaborate top-knot and tightened his silk belt around his waist.

The emperor sat behind a screen (for he was far too grand to be seen by ordinary people) to one side of the ring, and wished he were back inside the palace, reading poetry and sipping the finest tea. He hated wrestling and had only agreed to the match to please his bored and overdressed courtiers who had nothing better to do than gossip all day.

Mighty Mountain was just in time. A great gong was sounded and the match began. Mighty Mountain watched as the first two wrestlers prepared to enter the ring. There was a lot of bowing and stamping of huge flat feet, and then, throwing salt into the ring, the two men lurched towards each other. They were so fat that they just bounced off each other, right out of the ring. The emperor sighed.

Then it was Mighty Mountain's turn. As soon as he threw the salt and climbed into the ring, he stamped his mighty feet. The ground shook so much that his opponent, a very fat and red-faced man, was blown out of the ring. The next two wrestlers suddenly decided that it was not an auspicious day to fight and retreated out of sight. When the fourth man entered the ring, Mighty Mountain just picked him up with one hand and deposited him, none too gently, the other side of the rustling bamboo thickets. Another three competitors burst into tears and were taken away hurriedly. The ladies all giggled behind their fans as they looked properly at this handsome young man who seemed to have appeared from nowhere, yet who was quite the best wrestler ever seen at court.

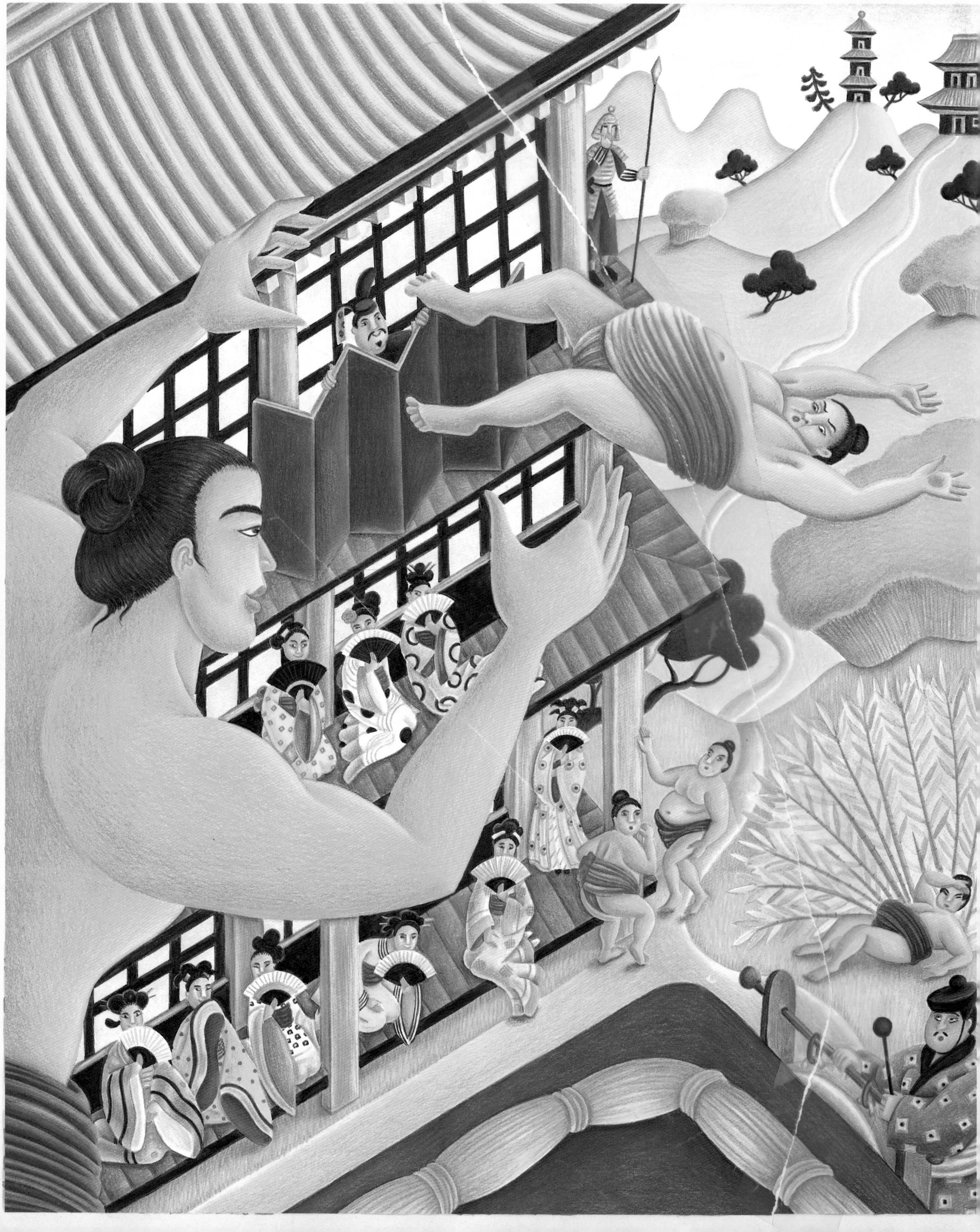

The emperor peeped from behind his screen. His face was solemn, but his eyes were brimming with laughter and his lacquered head-dress was shaking as he tried to maintain his dignity. He beckoned Mighty Mountain forward with his littlest finger (which was the very greatest honor for Mighty Mountain) and whispered, "Please take all the prize money and leave these useless opponents to eat their rice," and his voice quavered as he tried not to laugh.

A very superior-looking courtier, who was not laughing as he had just lost a great deal of money on the outcome of the Emperor's Wrestling Match, thrust a heavy bag of money at Mighty Mountain with scarcely an incline of his head. Mighty Mountain threw back his head and roared with laughter. Several of the court ladies fainted at the sound and the emperor's screen wobbled dangerously. It was time to go.

Mighty Mountain turned around and did not stop walking until he reached the bottom of the steep mountain track, and there coming down towards him was Kuniko! She looked at the bag of money and she looked at Mighty Mountain, and then she swept him, and the money, up into her arms and carried him all the way up the mountainside to Grandma and Mother. And there they all lived happily ever after. Grandma would still wrestle with Mighty Mountain, and sometimes she let him win. After all, he was the winner of the Emperor's Wrestling Match!

The Giant Sisters and the Silver Swan

Prince Locket lived with his parents, King Roland and Queen Rosalind the Fair, in a modest castle deep in an ancient forest. Spreading oak trees reached right up to the castle walls and wild boar rootled in the flower-strewn meadows that spread down to the river, splashing noisily over the rough stones that lay tumbled in the clear water. The castle had stout wooden gates but they were never closed as King Roland did not believe in pomp and ceremony. He always wanted his people to feel they could walk in whenever they wanted to see him, and discuss the weather or how best to cure a cow with hiccups.

The village well was a stone's throw from the gates and simple wooden cottages were huddled, all higgledy piggledy, around the marketplace. In one of these lived Lynnet, whose father was a cheesemaker. She often used to see Prince Locket as he went out with his sleek hunting dogs and a band of cheerful companions. Lynnet was a quiet girl but when she smiled her eyes crinkled in a most attractive way and she was possessed of a kind heart and great good sense.

One day, a very curious thing happened. As Prince Locket was riding home with his friends, a sudden and mysterious mist enveloped him, and him only. His friends were at first puzzled and then alarmed. When the mist lifted, as inexplicably as it had fallen, Prince Locket was nowhere to be seen. His friends shouted his name until they were hoarse, and the sleek hunting dogs ran around in ever-increasing circles, noses to the ground, but Prince Locket appeared to have vanished off the face of the earth. With heavy hearts, his friends sped back to the castle to break the dreadful news to King Roland and Queen Rosalind the Fair.

The king and queen were distraught. Prince Locket was their only son and they loved him dearly. Queen Rosalind the Fair took to her bed, the dark green velvet curtains drawn against the light, while the king wandered disconsolately around the market square, wringing his hands, with tears running down his face. Lynnet saw his grief and immediately decided, in her usual way, to do something practical. She put on her heavy clogs, wrapped a warm shawl around her shoulders and packed a little bag with one of her father's best cheeses and some freshly baked bread. She kissed her parents goodbye, telling them that she would find Prince Locket, however long it took her, and walked resolutely into the forest.

She walked for days along paths dappled with light as the sun filtered through the thick canopy of leaves. She drank water from the clear streams and, when her bread and cheese were finished, she ate the berries and nuts that she found along her way. Eventually, she came to the forest edge and before her lay a rocky valley. Curiously misshapen and stunted bushes clustered around a group of caves nearby, and the grass was all flattened as if a herd of raggedy sheep had trampled it down.

Dusk was falling, and so Lynnet decided to shelter in one of the caves for the night. The first one she looked in didn't smell very nice, and the second was full of damp moss, but the third looked dry and went back quite a way so Lynnet stepped in cautiously and looked around. The cave was large, but a tall glass of fireflies provided a soft light that reached even into the far corners. Something glittered in the gloom and when she tiptoed towards it, to her astonishment, Lynnet found two huge great beds, one covered with a silver quilt and one with a golden quilt. To her even greater astonishment, there, lying fast asleep on one of the huge beds, was Prince Locket. She called his name and, when there was no response, tried to climb up onto the bed to shake him awake. But the bed was so tall that she couldn't reach him. As she stood pondering how she might climb up, she noticed strange lettering carved around the bedhead. Lynnet could not read the words, which appeared to be in some ancient runic script.

As she gazed at the curious letters, she felt the ground begin to tremble beneath her feet and loud voices sounded outside the cave. She looked over her shoulder and there in the entrance stood two very big and very ugly giant women. Quick as a mouse, Lynnet slipped under one of the huge beds.

The giant women lumbered into the cave. "I can smell a human being," said one.

"Well, of course you can, stupid," said the younger of the two. "It's the prince, isn't it?" And they stumped over to the bed where Prince Locket lay.

Under the bed, Lynnet had a close-up view of four truly gigantic feet.

And then the giant women began to sing, in terrible cracked voices,

> Silver swan, silver swan, come swift as you may,
> For Locket must open his eyes straight away.

And into the cave flew a magnificent silver swan, swooping down to the end of the bed. Prince Locket immediately opened his eyes and sat up. He looked pale. The younger woman offered him food off a silver plate, but he would have none of it. Then, with a dreadful smile, she asked him if he would marry her.

"Certainly *not*," he said with great determination.

The giant women muttered angrily, "That is the only way you will ever be free, young Prince," and they cackled horribly, before singing again,

> Silver swan, silver swan, go swift as light.
> For Locket must close his eyes here tonight.

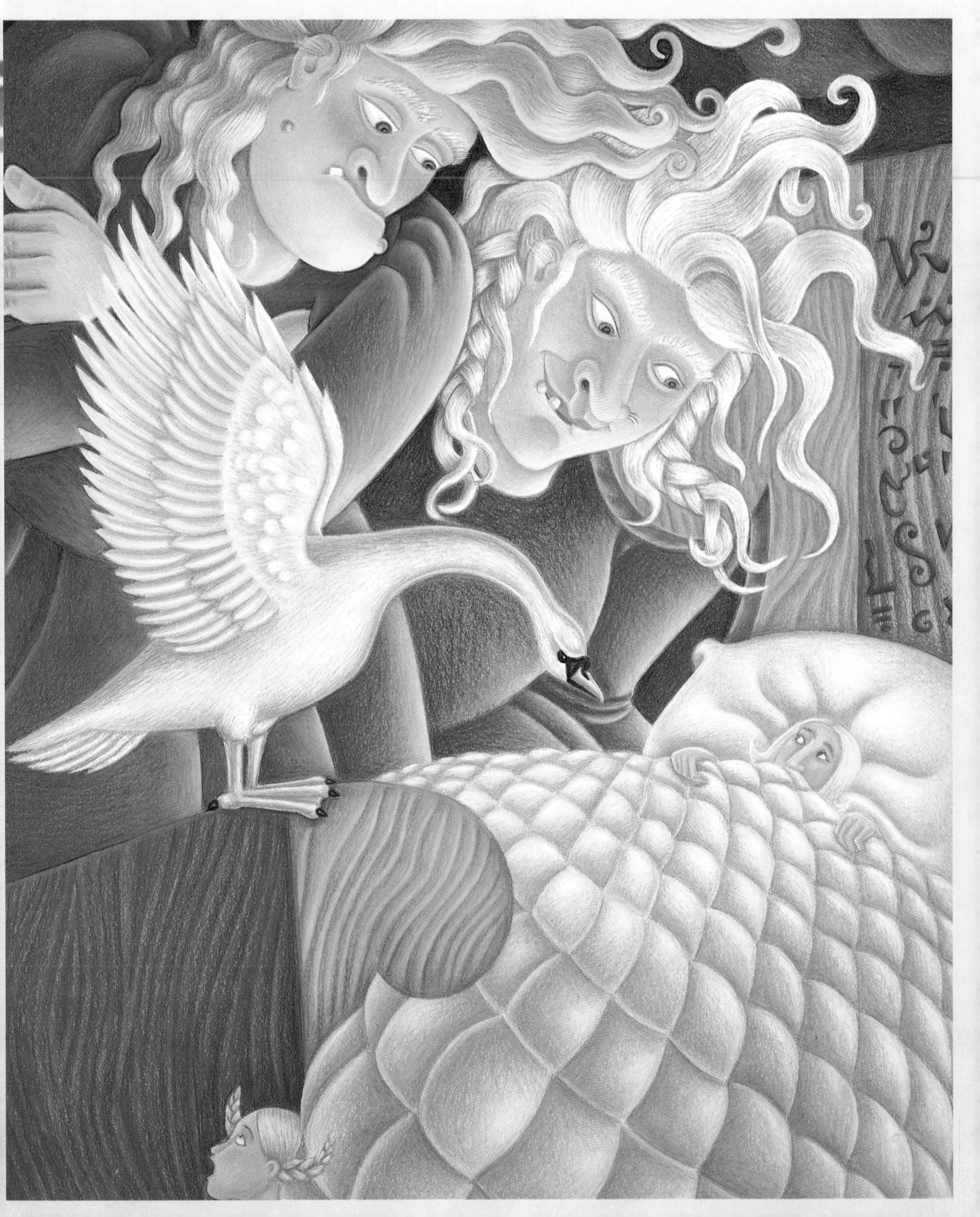

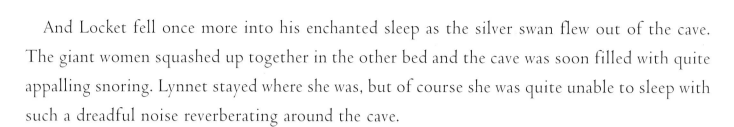

And Locket fell once more into his enchanted sleep as the silver swan flew out of the cave. The giant women squashed up together in the other bed and the cave was soon filled with quite appalling snoring. Lynnet stayed where she was, but of course she was quite unable to sleep with such a dreadful noise reverberating around the cave.

In the morning, the women rose with a great deal of grumbling and creaking of huge bones. "Have you got the speckled egg safely?" the younger one asked.

"Of course I have," replied the other crossly, and they stomped out of the cave.

After what seemed like an eternity, Lynnet decided it was safe enough to come out from her hiding-place. "Nothing ventured, nothing gained," she said to herself and, looking all the while at the sleeping Prince Locket, she repeated the verse she had memorized from the night before:

Silver swan, silver swan, come swift as you may,
For Locket must open his eyes straight away.

The silver swan flew into the cave and landed on the bed, its head cocked in surprise to see Lynnet. Instantly, Prince Locket sat up in bed. Great was his astonishment and delight when he saw Lynnet standing there. Questions tumbled out one after another as Lynnet tried to find out how Prince Locket came to be in the cave in the first place, and Prince Locket asked for news from home.

It transpired that the mist which had enveloped Prince Locket had been conjured up by the younger woman who wanted a husband to look after the cave while she and her sister were out during the day.

Lynnet thought for a while and then said to Prince Locket, "This is what we must do. Tonight when the giant woman asks you to marry her, you must agree—" At this point Prince Locket spluttered in protest but Lynnet carried on, "You must agree on condition that she tells you what she and her sister do all day." And with that she summoned the silver swan to put Prince Locket to sleep once more, crawled under the bed and fell fast asleep (for she was very tired of course, having been kept awake all night).

In the evening, the giant women came back and called the silver swan once more.

Silver swan, silver swan, come swift as you may,
For Locket must open his eyes straight away.

In flapped the magnificent swan, and landed on the end of the bed. Prince Locket immediately opened his eyes and sat up. The younger woman offered him food off a silver plate, but, as before, he would have none of it. Then, with a dreadful smile, she asked him again if he would marry her.

Trying very hard not to look at her tangled hair and her broken teeth and, worst of all, the huge wart at the end of her nose, Prince Locket said, "Certainly I will," with great determination.

At first the younger woman could not believe her ears, but when her sister thumped her on the back with a great whoop, she realized she had heard correctly. A ghastly smile crossed her face, revealing all her broken teeth, and Prince Locket crossed his fingers behind his back, hoping fervently that Lynnet knew what she was doing. "I will marry you," he repeated, "but you must tell me what you do all day."

"We hunt for food and then, when we have enough, we guard our speckled egg. It is our most precious possession for if it ever breaks we will die immediately."

Ah-hah, thought Lynnet, hiding under the bed.

The giant women ate a very hearty meal and then, having summoned the silver swan to put Prince Locket back to sleep once more, they tumbled into the other bed and were soon fast asleep, snoring deafeningly.

The next morning, the giant women summoned the silver swan as usual and when Prince Locket was awake, told him that they would leave him awake to explore if he chose. "Once we are married, you will be so busy you won't have time even to draw breath," grinned the younger woman in a most unattractive way and off they went out of the cave.

As soon as they were gone, Lynnet crept out from under the bed to join Prince Locket and the silver swan. "Silver swan, please help us," said Lynnet. "We need to escape from these terrible giant women. Can you help us?"

"Of course I can," murmured the swan and her voice was as soft as the wind in the reeds.

"You know that you must destroy the speckled egg. In the chest by the cave mouth you will find my silver bow and arrow. Take that, Prince Locket, and follow the giant women, and when they rest you will see that they lay the speckled egg down on a flat rock. You must take very careful aim indeed, for you will only have the one chance to hit it. As soon as you have done that you must come back here where Lynnet and I will be waiting for you."

Prince Locket needed no second bidding. He rushed to the great chest by the cave mouth and there indeed was the gleaming silver bow and arrow, lying on a sheepskin rug. He took it up carefully and, with a cheery wave, ran out of the cave after the women. Of course, one of their giant strides covered a great distance, so poor Prince Locket had to walk many miles before he heard a great rumbling sound. He had always been asleep himself when the women were asleep so he didn't know the rumbling sound was their snoring, but he soon came across them, stretched out on the grass, the speckled egg balanced on a flat rock nearby. Prince Locket drew back the silver bow very, very slowly and carefully, then let the arrow fly. Straight and true it went, and the speckled egg shattered with a mighty crack. Before Prince Locket's startled eyes, the giant women turned to stone and then crumbled to dust.

Meanwhile, back at the cave, the silver swan was explaining to Lynnet that that she had once been the familiar of a wonderful magician from the eastern lands, but she had been stolen by an ogre who was the father of the giant women. The great bed with the silver quilt had also belonged to the magician and the strange lettering carved around the bedhead was a spell to make it fly.

Under the sheepskin rug in the great chest where the silver bow and arrow had lain, Lynnet found a magnificent hoard of treasure. Bags of silver and gold coins, golden claret glasses, silver spoons and sparkling crowns of precious jewels lay jumbled together. As quickly as they could, the silver swan and Lynnet piled it all up on one of the beds and, in her voice soft as the wind in the reeds, the swan read out the spell written on the bed:

Turn around, turn around, great bed I implore,
Fly through the air and straight out the door.

The bed rose straight in the air and out of the cave, following the path the women's feet had worn in the grass. They soon found Prince Locket and he scrambled up onto the quilt and sat laughing with Lynnet among all the treasure. Lynnet then asked the bed very politely to fly them back home.

The silver swan flew alongside the bed, her great wings thrumming in the air. Soon the bed began to fly lower and dropped gently into the marketplace by the castle. Great was the rejoicing when the people saw Prince Locket and Lynnet both safely returned, and it was not long before King Roland himself heard all the commotion and came rushing up to hug his beloved son. Everyone was cheering and laughing, and, as the sound reached the queen's chamber, the dark green velvet curtains were drawn back. There stood Queen Rosalind the Fair, smiling joyfully at the window.

Prince Locket asked Lynnet to marry him, but she said she would rather travel the world on the magical bed. This she did often, a little bag with one of her father's best cheeses and some freshly baked bread by her side. The silver swan took up residence on the river by the flower-strewn meadows and was to be seen every evening, walking through the stout wooden gates into the castle to visit Prince Locket, King Roland and Queen Rosalind the Fair. So everyone lived happily ever after!

The Feathered Ogre

All the curtains were tightly drawn at the palace, the musicians were silent, the cooks stood idle in the kitchen and everyone tiptoed around in their slippers, for the king was very ill. The court physicians were utterly perplexed by the king's condition. All their potions and pills had failed to revive him, and now he was fading fast and likely to die. His favourite page boy, Fiore, went home to his mother, who was a Wise Woman, and told her sadly it looked likely that he would soon be looking for new employment.

"Well, it is obvious, isn't it?" she said straight away. "He needs a feather from the ogre."

It wasn't at all obvious to Fiore, of course, but his mother was never wrong about these things, so he asked her where he might find the ogre, for he loved his royal master very much and wanted to help however he might.

"If you follow the sun until it sets, you will find a wayside inn. Stay there for the night and then next day keep walking with the sun until you reach a wide river which you must cross. You will pass a fine gold and silver fountain, but keep walking until you reach the monastery at the foot of the mountain. Stay the night with the holy fathers and the next day you must climb the mountain. At the very top of the mountain you will find seven caves. The ogre lives in one of them. Some kindly soul will tell you which one, you may be sure of that," said his mother. And she quickly went and packed up some freshly baked bread and a slab of cheese and a spiced sausage.

Fiore was a bright boy, so he repeated all these instructions to himself as he bundled a warm blanket into his bag and then, kissing his mother on both cheeks, off he set.

Sure enough, as the sun set, he found the inn. It was a lonely spot and so the innkeeper was very glad of the company, and before too long Fiore was telling him all about his journey to find the ogre.

"If these feathers are so beneficial, you might get one for me, too," said the innkeeper. "And perhaps you could ask the ogre where my daughter is. She vanished seven long years ago."

Being an obliging boy, Fiore said he would.

In the morning he bid the innkeeper farewell and continued on his way. He walked and walked until he came to the river. It was indeed very wide and Fiore was just wondering how he would cross it when he heard the splash of oars, and there was the ferryman. As he rowed Fiore slowly across the river they talked, and before too long Fiore was telling him all about his journey to find the ogre.

"If these feathers are so beneficial, you might get one for me, too," said the ferryman. "And perhaps you could ask the ogre how I might get someone else to row this boat, I am getting old and tired."

Being an obliging boy, Fiore said he would.

Then he set off once more on his journey. He walked and walked until he came to the gold and silver fountain, just as his mother had told him. But no water came tumbling out of the fountain; it was quite dry. Still, Fiore had his own water bottle and it seemed a good place to rest, so he sat down to eat his lunch. Soon he was joined by two richly dressed noblemen and, as before, it was not long before Fiore was telling them all about his journey to find the ogre.

"If these feathers are so beneficial, you might get one for us, too," said the noblemen. "And perhaps you could ask the ogre why our glorious fountain has dried up."

Being an obliging boy, Fiore said he would.

Then he set off once more on his journey. He walked and walked until he came to the monastery. He rang the little bell hanging on the worn wooden door, and he was soon ushered in to the warmth of a huge fire with the holy fathers all clustered around him. It was a lonely spot and they were very glad of the company. Before too long, of course, Fiore was telling them all about his journey to find the ogre.

"Dear child, do you know what you have undertaken? This is a very fierce ogre. He will eat you up as soon as look at you. You had much better turn around and go straight back to your mother!" said the abbot.

Fiore was having none of that. "I am quite determined to try to save my king, and anyway I have made promises to all those people along the way," he said robustly. He was, as you know, an obliging boy.

"Pay attention then," said the abbot. "There are indeed seven caves at the top of the mountain. The last one is the ogre's but you must wait until noon before you go in. The ogre will be out then, up to no good you may be sure, but his wife will be there. She is a very kindly girl and why she stays with her horrible husband I will never know, but she will look out for you."

Fiore thanked the kindly abbot very much and retired to bed early, as he could see the next day was going to be difficult, not to mention dangerous.

In the morning, the abbot gave him a candle and some matches. "It will be very dark in the cave. Go carefully, my son, and be sure to tell us how you get on," he said, shaking his head sadly for, truth to tell, he did not expect to see Fiore ever again.

Fiore made tracks up the mountain, and hid himself carefully behind a large rock until it was noon. Then he strode boldly into the seventh cave. It was pitch dark inside, but he took out the abbot's candle and matches and found the gentle light very cheering as he made his way carefully to the back of the cave. In front of him there stood a huge wooden door with a great knocker in the shape of a very ugly face. Fiore was in no doubt that this was the ogre's front door.

He stood on tiptoe and raised the knocker. It took all his strength but it made a satisfying boom against the door, and he waited to see what might happen next.

A pretty girl opened the door and peered at him in horror. "Whatever are you doing here?" she cried. "Don't you know that a terrible ogre lives here and he will eat you up as soon as look at you?"

"I have come for some of his feathers," said Fiore. "If he eats me up, well at least I will have tried."

The pretty girl pulled Fiore inside and shut the door quickly. "My name is Melania and I am the ogre's wife. I can hide you under our bed and, when he is asleep, I will pull the feathers out one by one and pass them to you. How many do you want?"

And so Fiore told her all about the king and the innkeeper and the ferryman and the two noblemen, and he told her their questions as well.

"You are clearly a very obliging boy," she said with a sad smile. "Perhaps you can help me, too. I don't know how I came to be here and I would dearly love to escape."

"We will leave together, tomorrow morning, when I have my four feathers and my answers!" said Fiore confidently.

And so Melania hid Fiore under the great four-poster bed. Then she began to cook the ogre's supper. Fiore lay quiet as a mouse. Soon he felt the ground shake, and then the door crashed open—with a bellow, the ogre had come home.

"I smell a human being!" he roared.

"Nonsense!" said Melania. "You are imagining things. Sit down and eat your supper, I have roasted a whole ox specially for you."

So the ogre ate his supper, still snuffling the air suspiciously and stamping his feet. But eventually the food and warmth began to make him sleepy and before long Fiore felt the great bed dip as the ogre lay down with a big sigh. He was soon asleep, and snoring most dreadfully.

Melania looked under the bed and smiled at Fiore, then she too climbed up onto the bed.

"Ouch!" yelled the ogre suddenly.

"Oh, my dear husband, I am so sorry. I was dreaming about the fountain below our mountain and I must have pulled out one of your feathers," said Melania, as her hand slipped over the side of the mattress and she passed a feather to Fiore.

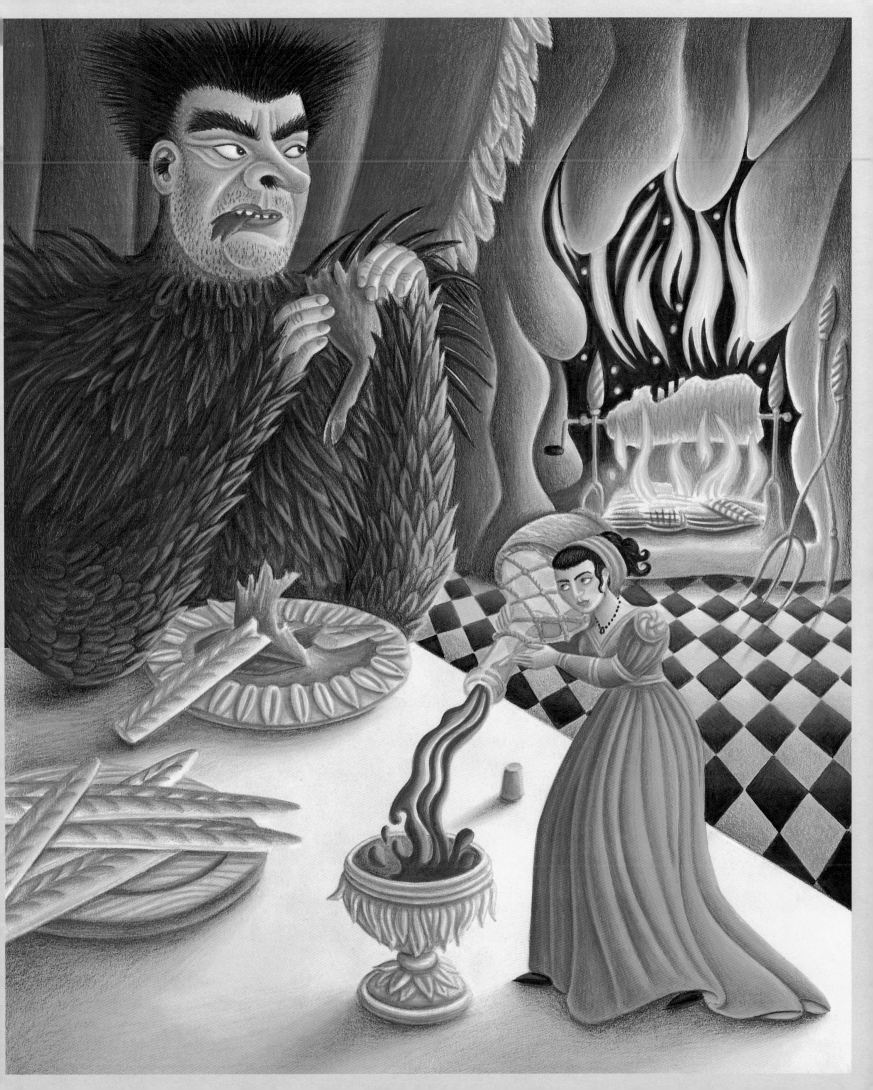

"Why were you dreaming about the fountain?" muttered the ogre as he tried to get comfortable again.

"It was so strange," said Melania. "I dreamed it had run dry."

"It has indeed run dry," said the ogre crossly. "There is a great snake curled up around the spout," and he went back to sleep.

Before too long the ogre gave another shout, "Another of my feathers! What is wrong with you?"

"I was dreaming again," Melania said humbly. "I am so sorry, my husband. But I was dreaming about the ferryman down on the wide river in the next valley. He hasn't been able to stop working for years," and as she spoke, Melania passed another feather down to Fiore.

"The man is a fool," snorted the ogre. "He only has to jump off the boat before his next passenger, and the passenger will then have to become the ferryman. Now let me sleep, wife," and he pulled the blankets close and went back to sleep.

Fiore waited a long time in the dark. Perhaps Melania had fallen asleep herself? But no, she did not let him down.

With a great bellow, the ogre suddenly sat up in bed. "Wife! You have pulled out two of my feathers this time! Now what are you dreaming about?" and he was very angry indeed.

"My dear husband, I am so very sorry. This time I was dreaming about the poor innkeeper where the sun sets. He has lost his only daughter these seven long years and he misses her sorely," sobbed Melania who seemed greatly affected by her sad dream. But she still managed to pass the feathers to the delighted Fiore.

"Foolish woman! You are the innkeeper's daughter," shouted the ogre. "I found you seven years ago when I was out hunting, and, as I needed someone to look after me, I biffed you on the head so you would forget to go home. Now let there be no more interruptions or I shall be forced to eat you for breakfast," and the ogre banged his pillows in a great rage and tossed and turned before finally falling asleep once again.

Fiore and Melania knew they had not a moment to hesitate. Clutching the feathers tightly in one hand and guiding the trembling Melania with the other, Fiore fled back through the cave. They tumbled helter-skelter down the mountainside in their haste and ran as fast as ever they could to the monastery. They rang the little bell hanging on the worn wooden door, and told the delighted abbot that all had gone well with them so far, but that as soon as he awoke, the ogre would no doubt be in hot pursuit. The abbot waved them on their way with his heartfelt blessing and then set all the holy fathers to barricading the door against the ogre.

On and on Fiore and Melania sped, and soon they reached the fountain. Fiore gave the two noblemen the feather, and Melania told them about the great snake curled around the spout. Sure enough there it was, but as soon as they had uncoiled the snake and flung it far into the meadows, the fountain began to cascade again. The two noblemen showered Fiore and Melania with bags of gold and called their grateful thanks down the road after them.

And still the two walked on until they came to the wide river, and there was the ferryman, as ever, patiently taking his passengers to and fro. "Here is your feather," said Fiore with a smile.

"And how am I to be relieved of my duties as ferryman?"

"I will tell you once we have reached the other side," said Fiore cautiously. And once both he and Melania were safely on dry land, Fiore told the ferryman exactly how he could be released.

By now they were both very tired and the inn was a welcome sight as they walked down the road towards the setting sun. Of course the innkeeper was overjoyed to see Melania again, and full of gratitude to Fiore. "You will be very welcome to stay here whenever you wish," he said, laughing and crying at the same time.

The next morning, Fiore was up bright and early, as he was now anxious to get to the king in time. He and Melania bid each other a fond farewell, and she and her father watched his retreating figure all the way down the road until he was no longer to be seen. The innkeeper put the ogre's feather in a safe place, and, with Melania's share of the gold from the two noblemen, he set about restoring the inn which had become very run down in the seven years he had been all on his own. Soon it looked very welcoming and, as Melania was so pretty too, it was not long before the inn was filled with young men all anxious to attract her attention. Of course they drank a great deal of wine which made the innkeeper very happy—and very rich—and so he and his daughter lived very happily ever after.

Fiore did not even pause to visit his mother but made his way straight to the palace. The king was not expected to last until the evening, but Fiore pushed his way into the royal bedchamber and laid the ogre's feather on the counterpane. He held his breath and waited. Slowly, the colour came back into the king's cheeks and it was not too long before he was sitting up in bed demanding a boiled egg and toast. And he lived for many years to come, always looked after by his favourite page boy, Fiore.

Every Sunday, Fiore would visit his mother. With his blessing, for he was an obliging boy, she used some of Fiore's gold from the two noblemen to plant a fine herb garden and her fame as a healer spread far and wide. Fiore himself used the rest of the gold to buy a magnificent horse for he had developed quite a taste for travelling, after his quest for the ogre's feathers. He would gallop for miles and miles, always in quite the opposite direction to the ogre's cave, however.

And what of the ogre, you might ask? Well, he was in a fine rage when he woke to find Melania had run away, so he set off in pursuit, quite determined to make her his next meal. He huffed and puffed his way to the wide river where he ordered the ferryman to take him across as fast as possible, but as soon as the boat reached the other side, the ferryman leapt out with a cry of delight and the ogre was left behind to act as ferryman forever. For all I know, he is there still.

Small Abdul, the Ogress and the Caliph's Daughter

Along time and a time ago, there lived a devout Muslim called Big Abdul. He was very tall and possessed enormous strength, but he was a gentle man; a generous husband to his wife, Fatima; and a kindly father to his little son, Small Abdul. Now Small Abdul was not called this merely because he was young, for Small Abdul did not take after his big father. He was tiny, no larger than a doll, but he had a stout heart and his parents were devoted to him.

A time came when the family wanted to make a pilgrimage to Mecca, so Fatima packed all the provisions they would need for the journey and they set off with many other pilgrims in a winding caravan of camels. But as they were nearing the end of their long journey, the caravan was set upon by a band of fierce brigands. The menfolk were scattered or, much worse, left to die by the wayside, while the women were borne away on the fastest camels, their children clutched fearfully in their arms. The brigands had grown tired of the filthy state of their camp and were looking to the women to cook and clean and wash their clothes.

At the brigands' camp, years went by. Time passed slowly. Fatima worked as hard as any of the other women, but Small Abdul was always looking for ways to escape. Being so small, he was able to creep about unobserved. He discovered that the brigands had a huge treasure store of stolen gold and silver, but it was very firmly under lock and key. They did, however, also have a vast stable of camels and it was here that Small Abdul thought the escape route lay for Fatima and himself.

One dark night, the raiding party of brigands came back with an exceptionally fine string of camels. The very best of these beasts was a mehari, a racing camel, and Small Abdul realized this was the chance he and Fatima had been waiting for. No other creature would be able to catch up with the mehari once it was loose. Soon the brigands were snoring after the huge meal Fatima and the other women had prepared, so Small Abdul slipped into the stable and untied the mehari. It snorted and kicked a bit, for camels are not the most equable of beasts, but Small Abdul whispered all kinds of nonsense into its ear and the snooty beast was so taken aback that it knelt down in the sand to allow Fatima and Small Abdul to climb up onto its swaying back. The moon came up and the mehari sped across the desert as fast and as wild as the wind.

The mehari knew exactly where it was going, back to the wealthy sheikh it had been stolen from, and it did not pause until dusk the following day when it knelt down in front of the sheikh's tent. Sore and utterly weary, Fatima and Small Abdul slid off the camel and bowed very low to the fierce-looking sheikh who had come out of his tent to see what all the commotion was about. Fatima nervously and very quickly explained what had happened, for the sheikh's eyebrows were drawing together in rage. But as soon as he heard their story, the sheikh ushered Fatima and Small Abdul into the comfort of his tent where he plied them with sweetmeats and refreshing sherbet, so delighted was he to see his mehari back again. And even as Fatima and Small Abdul sipped their sherbet, a troop of the sheikh's finest warriors were on their way to the brigands' camp to rescue the rest of the valuable camels and, I am sure you will be pleased to hear, to rescue all the other women who had been forced into working for the grubby band of ruffians.

The sheikh was profuse in his thanks to Small Abdul for the return of his favourite mehari, who, it turned out, was a beast of exceptionally high value as well as being so fleet of foot.

"Thousandfold is my gratitude to you, O Small, but very brave, Abdul. I would deem it an extraordinary favor were you and your esteemed mother to reside with me here. You, Small Abdul, would be treated as one of my sons and your mother would be cared for as well as one of my many wives," he smiled, his dark eyes twinkling.

"My revered mother and I are very honored by your generosity but we have a great desire to find our way home to discover if Big Abdul, a thousand blessings on his head, is still alive," said Small Abdul, bowing very low.

"Then I insist that you accept the young camel born last spring to my noble mehari, the same camel that you have brought home safely to me, as a token of my undying gratitude to you," said the sheikh.

Small Abdul was overwhelmed by the magnificence of the sheikh's present; such a beast would have been way beyond his means. Now he would have not only the fleetest-footed beast imaginable, but he would be able to take his mother home safely, for the options were limited for one so small in a world of brigands and thieves.

So after a magnificent feast lasting several days and nights, Small Abdul and Fatima set off home to see what they might find. Five long years had passed since the family had all embarked on their pilgrimage, and Fatima feared in her darkest thoughts that if Big Abdul was still alive it was entirely possible that he had taken another wife, if not three or four, as was his right under the Muslim law.

But as soon as they rode into town and stopped in front of their old home, Big Abdul rushed out, his eyes filled with tears of joy. "How wonderful are the ways of the mighty Allah! My family restored to me after all these weary years of waiting," and he hugged Fatima and then Small Abdul and then Fatima all over again. He admired the camel—who, truth to tell, was casting a rather superior look around Big Abdul's humble home—and then ushered his precious family indoors (where there were no new wives waiting to upset Fatima!) and bade them tell him all about the missing five years. He himself had been badly wounded by the brigands and had wandered for days, growing ever weaker, until a passing physician took pity on him and healed his wounds. The physician was never able to heal his heart, however, which was overwhelmed by the loss of his beloved Fatima and the plucky Small Abdul.

And there you might think the story ends, with the family happily reunited, but fate had another hand to deal Small Abdul. Years passed, and the young camel grew longer in the legs and as fast as a whirling sandstorm. Small Abdul did not grow an inch, but his reputation as a solver of problems did. Many great and mighty warriors and wealthy sheikhs came to Small Abdul's humble house to use his tiny size but clever brain to regain lost treasure or to find missing animals or to return wandering wives, and Small Abdul's stable of camels grew commensurate with their gratitude.

One day a terrible thing happened. The only daughter of the caliph, the Lady Akila, was stolen away by an ogress of terrible reputation. She stood as tall as a dust storm and was twice as ugly as a warthog. Her hair hung in filthy rats-tails down her back, and dirt was encrusted under her talons. Her skin was swart and as wrinkled as an elephant, and her eyes were coal black with red pupils that glittered in the dark. She wore a dented breastplate and carried a notched scimitar, and she had a two-sided axe thrust in her belt. You could smell her coming from quite a distance. She lived in a huge palace where the topmost towers were lost in the clouds. There was a massive wooden door to this palace, bound with bands of steel and

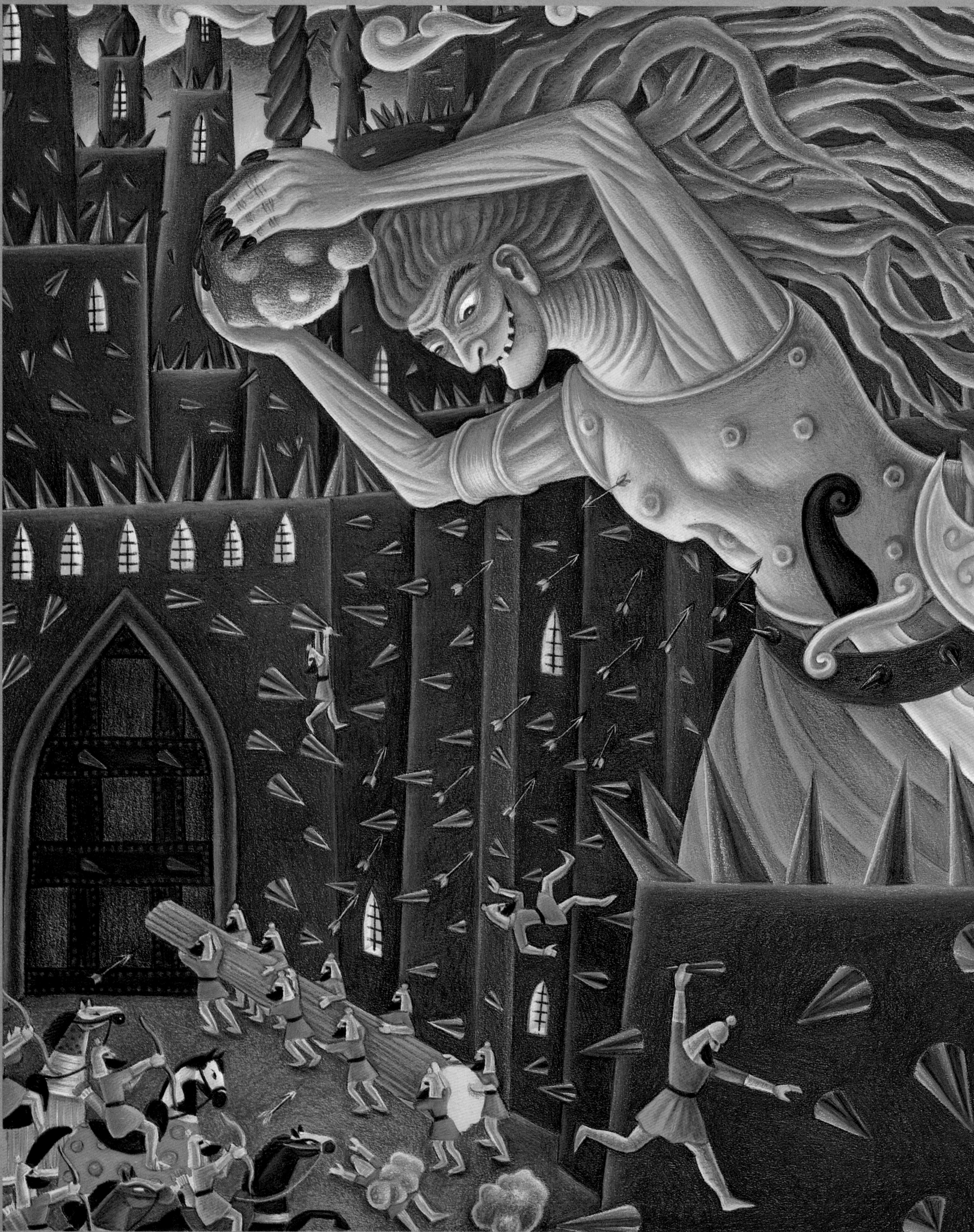

surrounded by iron-grilled windows, suitable for pouring boiling oil down on the head of anyone foolish enough to mount an attack on the ogress. The Lady Akila could not have fallen into worse hands.

The caliph sent his fiercest warriors in a vast army to attack the palace, but the ogress just laughed and picked the warriors off one by one as they tried in vain to scale the great walls of the palace. A huge battering ram failed even to dent the steel bands of the massive wooden door, and when the ogress herself appeared, a dark hail of arrows just glanced off her horrible skin. Her eyes flared with delight as she hefted several boulders down onto the dismayed warriors who were forced into an ignominious retreat. When the caliph heard the news, he flung a black robe about his head and wept for his dear daughter whom he thought he had now lost forever.

Small Abdul was in the stables with his greatly pampered camels when his mother came running in, calling his name excitedly. She had just returned from the bazaar. "Small Abdul, Small Abdul, stop fussing over those dratted animals and go to the caliph immediately. He has great need of your guile and cunning. The Lady Akila has been stolen away by a fearful ogress!"

Small Abdul wasted no time in saddling up his fastest camel and galloped with all due haste to present himself to the caliph. I am sorry to say the caliph had not heard of Small Abdul's prowess, and so, when he looked down at the diminutive figure who appeared to be offering to rescue his daughter where his mighty army had failed, he just snorted and said, "You dare to go where my mighty warriors have failed? You are either very foolish or a magician. Either way, if you can restore my daughter to me, which I very much doubt, if you can restore my daughter to me, I shall, of course, be very grateful to you. Now go away and leave the rescuing of the Lady Akila to those better able to do so!"

Small Abdul was not at all put out by this rude response. Many people before the caliph had failed to appreciate his abilities. Small Abdul bowed very low, walked out of the throne room backwards (which is how you have to behave in the presence of a caliph, however rude he might be), mounted his camel once again and made his way towards the palace whose topmost towers were lost in the clouds.

The ogress, satisfied that she had disposed of the caliph's warriors for the meantime, had gone back inside. As the camel knelt in front of the massive wooden door, Small Abdul slipped off quietly and listened carefully. He could hear a great rumbling sound like distant thunder.

Small Abdul frowned and then he smiled. The sound was snoring: the ogress was fast asleep.

"Excellent!" Small Abdul murmured to himself and he wriggled through the iron grille of one of the windows. He dropped, as quietly as a moth, onto the stone floor which was rather revoltingly strewn with the bones of earlier victims of the ogress. Small Abdul followed the sound of snoring up the filthy stairs and found himself in a vast room with a pile of animal skins in one corner. Upon this lay the ogress, her great mouth open. There was no sign of the notched scimitar, nor the two-sided axe. Small Abdul crept as close as he could bear, what with the snoring and the smell, and then he blew very hard into the ogress's left nostril.

She awoke with a great start and bellowed, "I smell a filthy human being! Who has dared trespass into my palace?" and she looked all around the room. But Small Abdul was so small that she couldn't see him under her great warty chin. He hopped down and rolled a few convenient skulls into the middle of the room, and, as the ogress lumbered to her feet and made for the door, she tripped over the skulls and lost her balance. With a fearful crash she fell through the door and tumbled all the way down the stairs, head over heels, over and over. When she reached the bottom she lay very still indeed. Small Abdul made his way carefully down after her. To his great delight and enormous relief, she was dead, her thick neck broken in the fall. So that was the end of her.

Small Abdul then set out to find the Lady Akila. He searched the great palace from top to bottom, and in the very last room of all he found the terrified caliph's daughter, all trussed up like a chicken. She was obviously intended for the ogress's next meal. After he had assured her that the ogress really was dead, Small Abdul led the trembling Lady Akila downstairs and out into the keep behind the massive wooden door. There he persuaded her to stand tiptoe on his shoulders so she could reach the huge key in the lock (for he was too small to perform this feat on his own) and with a struggle the Lady Akila turned it and the door creaked open. Small Abdul peered around the door. Ranged outside were the caliph's warriors, at least those few who had survived the first attack on the palace.

"You must go out first, my lady," said Small Abdul very politely to the Lady Akila. "Your father's warriors are outside and I think they are looking for you."

As soon as the Lady Akila put her dainty foot outside the massive wooden door, a great shout of joy came from all the warriors. Her nurse came rushing up and pulled her away from the castle as if all the djinns in the outer darkness were behind her. The warriors turned about to escort their precious passenger back to the caliph, and soon all that Small Abdul could see was a retreating cloud of dust.

He made his way home slowly and went straight away to the stable to pick stones out of his camel's tender feet and to see she was fed and watered after their long gallop home. Then he went quietly to bed and was soon deep in a dreamless sleep.

But Small Abdul was awoken just as the sun rose by a great hubbub outside his window. Big Abdul and Fatima came rushing in, both speaking at once in their excitement.

"The caliph, the caliph wants you to go—" said Fatima

"—to the palace at once because the Lady Akila says—" shouted Big Abdul.

"—that you rescued her!" finished Fatima, and they both looked expectantly at Small Abdul.

"Bother!" said Small Abdul. " I was rather hoping to try my newest mehari out today."

Of course Fatima prised the truth out of him and before he really had time to draw breath, Small Abdul was washed and scrubbed and on his way to the caliph.

Now, it is normal in such circumstances to offer the hand of the rescued maiden in marriage to the mighty warrior as a reward. But then Small Abdul was not a mighty warrior, and the caliph was afraid his daughter would look ridiculous with such a small husband. Anyway, as it happened, Small Abdul had no desire to live in the palace with so many servants and ceremonial horns blowing all day, enough to give you a very bad headache. So the caliph bestowed the highest honor (after the Lady Akila that is) on Small Abdul by giving him a lion's heart robe of honor. The caliph was not a little embarrassed by his earlier treatment of Small Abdul, and so, in addition, he was given not only *his* weight in gold (which would not have been very much at all) but the weight of Big Abdul and Fatima as well, and that was a great deal of gold!

Small Abdul built a fine house on the outskirts of the city so his camels could race over the desert to their heart's content, and he and Big Abdul and Fatima lived in great contentment together for many years.

How Coyote Escaped from the Giant

He was a tricky customer, Coyote. He was forever meddling and making mischief. But never did the mud stick to his paws. Coyote sometimes appeared as an animal and sometimes as a human and this made him very tricky indeed. The animal Coyote was small and cunning, and he looked a bit like a jackal. He had very sharp teeth and a thick brush of a tail, tipped with black. The human Coyote could take on any shape that he chose and he had many disguises. He brought fire and light to his people. He set the moon and the sun and the stars in their rightful places, and he created the horse and gave the bear his small tail. But mainly he caused trouble.

One day he was prowling around, singing tunelessly to himself, when he met an old woman. She did not recognize Coyote and so did not realize who she was dealing with. "I would be careful if I were you," she said as Coyote slid past her (he had not thought her worth the bother of eating).

"Why should I be careful, old woman?" demanded Coyote, not a little offended by her failure to recognize him for the mighty hero he thought he was.

"I would be careful if I were you because there is a great giant up ahead, and he will eat you up as soon as look at you," said the old woman.

"I am not afraid of a mere giant," snarled Coyote, who actually had no idea what a giant was.

"You should be afraid of this one," said the old woman. "His eyes are like huge dark suns and his mouth is as wide as a cave."

Coyote sneered at the old woman and he carried on in the same direction as before. But once he was a little way around the corner and out of her sight, he bent down and picked up a huge fallen branch to use as a club. "Just in case," he said to himself as he walked on.

Soon he came to a wide canyon. Steep white cliffs rose either side and there was a red, dried-up riverbed running away into the distance. Coyote walked on for quite a way. There was a crunching sound beneath his feet and when he looked down he saw that the ground was covered in bleached white bones. "How strange," thought Coyote. "I am walking along a highway of bones."

Then up ahead he saw an emaciated man, sitting on a huge pile of skulls. "Help me," whispered the man in a voice as thin as a reed. "I am dying of hunger."

Coyote rummaged around in his medicine bag and produced some pemmican, a kind of cake made from dried meat and fat and berries, which he always carried with him. The man stuffed as much as he could all into his mouth at once as if his very life depended on it, which indeed it probably did, figured Coyote. After a while Coyote asked very casually, "You haven't by any chance seen a giant around these parts, have you?"

The man gave a shriek of what might have been laughter, but then he turned to Coyote and said, very seriously, "What kind of fool are you? Of course I have seen the giant. We are both sitting in his belly!"

Coyote was utterly horrified and looked around in a panic.

"You probably thought you were just walking through a canyon back awhiles, but that is actually the giant's mouth. The cliffs are his teeth and the red, dried-up riverbed is his tongue," said the man, still eating as if his life depended on it. Coyote snatched the precious pemmican back and sat down with a thump.

"We must go back as fast as we can and leave through his mouth again then!" cried Coyote.

"Too late," said the man. "Look over your shoulder. There is no light at the end of the canyon, the giant has closed his mouth."

Now this was a pretty poor fix to be in, Coyote thought, but he was very tricky and he knew

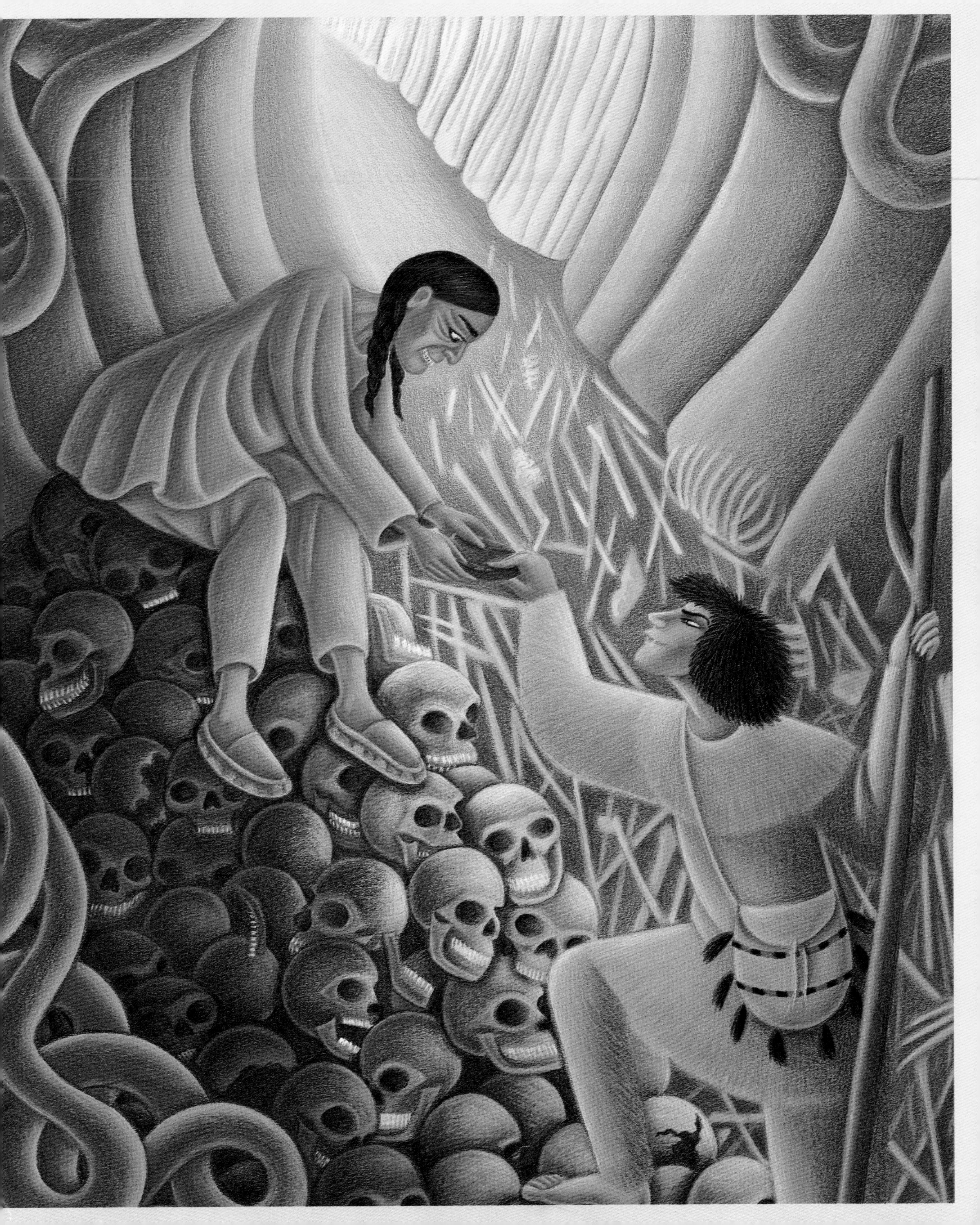

there must be a way out. "What are those great coils hanging from the sides of the canyon?" he asked.

"That is the inside of the giant's stomach," said the man.

Coyote thought about that for a while, and then he took out his hunting knife and, leaping up onto the great coils, carved out a huge slice that he threw down to the man. "We can eat our way out," Coyote said triumphantly.

"What a clever idea!" said the man.

"I am tricky," said Coyote. "I think of things like that."

Coyote swung his way along the great coils towards a great dark hummock that was pounding away like a tom-tom. It was the giant's heart. Coyote slithered closer and closer and then reached over and plunged his knife into the tip of the heart. There was a mighty rushing sound and a roar.

"Is that you, Coyote?" said a loud booming voice.

At last, thought Coyote, someone who knows just who I am.

"Yes, it is I, Coyote, the greatest and most tricky creature you will ever meet!" yelled Coyote.

"Please stop all this hacking and cutting at once. I shall open my mouth and you can leave immediately," rumbled the giant.

"See," said Coyote to the man, "I am tricky, I will get us out of here." He swung back down to the bone-strewn floor and walked towards the ever-growing light as the giant opened his huge mouth. And so the man and Coyote walked out of the canyon that was the giant's mouth, through the steep white cliffs that were the giant's teeth, and past the red, dried-up riverbed that was the giant's tongue. The man was afraid of Coyote—even though he had just rescued him—and so he made a very deep bow and then ran away as fast as if all the giants in the land were after him.

Coyote sniggered and then picked his paws. "Hah!" he grinned. "I am tricky, and now I have defeated a giant! Surely there is no creature left who can outwit me," and, full of similar conceited thoughts, he shouldered his medicine bag and continued on his way.

Coyote still roams the plains and he is still as tricky as ever, so be very careful if you meet a small wolf-like creature with very sharp teeth and a thick brush of a tail, tipped with black. But then he might be in his human form, and you will not know you have met him until he cheats you.

He is a tricky customer, that Coyote.

Thor Visits the Land of the Giants

Thor, the thunder-maker, was the god of war. He was terrible to behold as he hefted his mighty hammer, Mjollnir, and no matter how far he might fling it, the huge hammer would always return straight to his hand. He could split a mountain clean in two with one blow, he could uproot an entire forest with one hand and his pride was as great as his strength, but even a mighty god can be humbled, as you shall see.

Thor had grown weary of guarding Asgard, the home of the gods, for there were no battles to win and no one to challenge his huge strength, so he decided to visit Utgard, the land of the giants.

"Let me come with you," whined Loki, the trickster, who was also bored with the quiet life in Asgard. "You could do with some brains in the land of the giants," he sniggered, for although he was no match for Thor's strength, his wits were as sharp as the keenest sword. Thor gave him a thunderous look, but truth to tell, Thor was an uncomplicated man, not at all wily and easily bested by the magical arts. "Perhaps I might use his resourcefulness," thought Thor to himself, and so the following day the two set off together towards Utgard.

Long they walked across the wide plain, and it was dusk before they reached the mighty gates of Utgard. The walls were so high that even Thor could not see over the top, and the gates were made of wide bars of iron. While Thor looked at the gates with a deep frown between his eyes, pondering where the weak spot might be, Loki slipped through the bars easily and, once safely on the other side, made faces at Thor. "See! You need tricks as well as strength," he said gleefully.

This so enraged Thor, whose temper was not improved by the sight of several giants also laughing at him from behind the gates, that he strode up to the gates and, with a burst of his huge strength, bent two bars back sufficiently to allow him to wriggle through. This was not the dignified and awe-inspiring entrance that Thor had planned. However, he huffed up his shoulders, cuffed Loki around the ears and demanded of the watching giants that he be taken to the king, Utgard-Loki.

The sneering giants deputed a passing servant to the job as further proof of their contempt for Thor, and so it was with a lowering scowl that Thor strode angrily into the great hall. Smoke from a vast fire of what looked like whole trees curled upwards through a hole in the roof. Huge shaggy goats scuffed around in the dirty straw on the rough earthen floor, and chickens the size of dogs sat on the great cross-beams of the roof and fluffed their feathers. And everywhere there were mighty giants, men and women, and even children, sprawled on the floor by the fire or stretched out on vast benches around a long table, covered in food at varying stages of consumption. Bones littered the floor and savage dogs slavered and snarled at each other as they fought over the debris. Loki sniffed audibly. Silence fell abruptly as Thor made his way through the hall to the fireside.

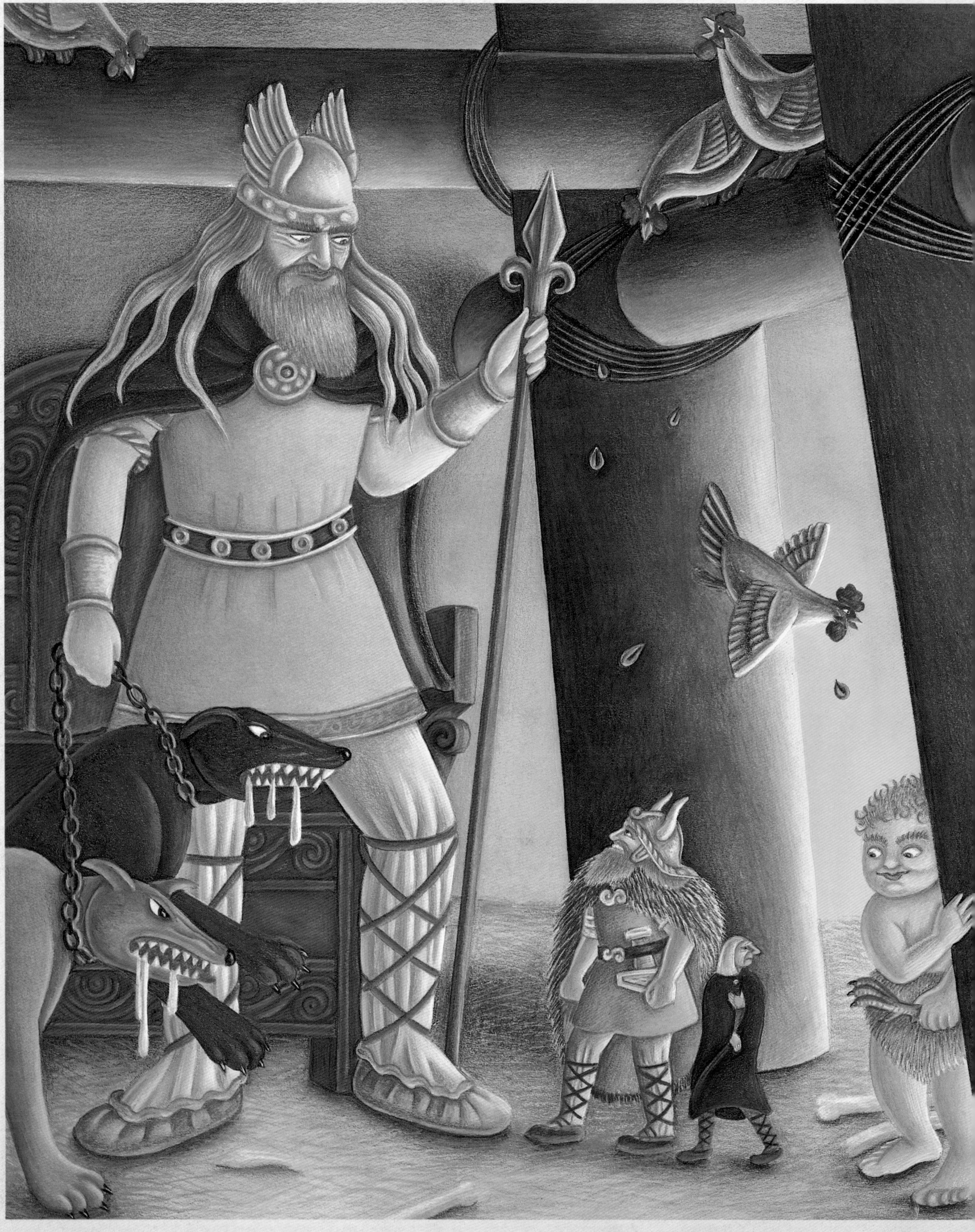

"Greetings to you and yours. My name is…" began Thor.

"Thor," interjected a huge figure sitting in a colossal wooden chair, just visible in the dim light at the far end of the hall. "Thor, the Charioteer," the voice repeated. "I know just who you are, you and your overly fastidious companion."

The speaker rose. It was Utgard-Loki himself, the king of Utgard, and he was truly a giant. He planted his massive legs apart and looked over the top of Thor's head in contempt. "Can this really be the mighty Thor? Perhaps he is stronger than he looks. Anyone who wishes to sit at my table has to prove himself first. What can you and your … what exactly is he, a henchman? What skills do you and your companion possess?"

Loki could see Thor was brewing up to an almighty bellow of rage which he felt might not be in their best interests so, although bridling at the "henchman" jibe, he quickly spoke up. Loki said, "I have a certain ability to eat anyone else under the table and I am famished after our journey here today. Perhaps I might demonstrate?" and Loki swept his hand around the room in a contemptuous challenge.

Utgard-Loki bared his teeth in an unpleasant smile. "I see the henchman is bold, Thor. Too bold, he shall regret his rash challenge. Very well then, let the contest begin," and he beckoned a young giant whose name was Logi to come forward. The servants brought in a huge trencher piled high with meat which they placed between Loki and Logi. Loki smiled and began to gobble the meat. In no time at all, the two contestants met in the middle. Loki had indeed consumed an incredible amount, but to his consternation, Logi had eaten all the bones and the trencher as well.

"A win to Utgard, I think," said Utgard-Loki, roaring with laughter. Loki skulked back to Thor, seething.

"My turn, I think," muttered Thor to Loki. "I doubt anyone here can drink as much as I can," he declaimed in ringing tones.

A huge drinking horn was brought in. Now a drinking horn can not be put down when it is full so it has to be drunk in one gulp. Thor did not think he would have any difficulty as he began drinking, but, to his dismay, the level of water in the horn did not appear to be getting lower. He strove to hold his breath, but he could manage no more.

"Quite a good try, but nowhere near enough, do you want to try again?" grinned Utgard-Loki.

Thor peered into the drinking horn in mighty puzzlement. The level had gone down a little so he raised it to his lips once more. But yet again he was defeated. He was angry with himself for he could not imagine why he was unable to do what he had done many times before. For a third time he raised the drinking horn to his lips, but for a third time he spluttered to a stop, the horn still half full.

"Perhaps you are tired after your journey, Thor?" suggested Utgard-Loki unhelpfully. "I could always propose another test: you could lift my cat off the ground for instance. I hesitate to ask the mighty Thor to perform such a slight feat, but it amuses my young giants here."

At his words, a gray cat slid out from under his chair. This was no kitten but a creature the size of a lion. Thor, his brows drawn together in a deep frown of irritation, took a step forward and crooked his arm under the cat. The cat arched her back. Thor put his other arm around her shoulders and pulled. The cat arched her back further, but all her four paws remained firmly on the floor. Thor stepped right up and placed both his feet under her belly, tightened his grasp and tugged with all his might. The sinews in his neck stood out as he strained but all he managed was to get the cat to lift one paw.

"Never mind, Thor," said Utgard-Loki silkily, "she is rather a big cat." And all the giants in the hall echoed his mocking laughter.

By now Thor was in a towering rage. He glared at all the laughing giants, and flung Mjollnir on the floor. "I will wrestle any man here!" he hissed, spitting the words out through clenched teeth. "The mighty Thor is not afraid!"

Utgard-Loki smiled, "Of course you are not afraid, mighty Thor," but his face belied his words. "I shall find you someone to wrestle with. Of course you must understand that it would be beneath any of my companions to wrestle with you, but I know my old nurse Elli would greatly enjoy such a competition," and he called for Elli to be brought into the hall.

This was the ultimate insult to Thor, to wrestle with a woman, and an old one at that! And when Elli hobbled into the hall, his humiliation was complete. For Elli was an ancient and wrinkled old crone who could only walk with the aid of a stick.

"I refuse to wrestle with an old woman!" blustered Thor, but Elli was having none of it. She threw away her stick and took up her position in front of the angry god, then hurled herself at him. As soon as he took hold of her, Thor knew he was defeated. She was much stronger than she looked and she was very speedy on her feet. Thor struggled bravely for as long as he could, but, with a sudden feint, Elli caught him unawares and forced him down onto one knee.

"Enough!" called out Utgard-Loki. "You have tried your best, Thor, but clearly that is not enough."

Thor picked up Mjollnir once again and hefted its weight in his hand. But his confidence was badly dented. Even if he was to fling Mjollnir with all his strength, who was to say what effect it might have. Would some young giant merely catch it in one hand as if it were a willow twig? He scowled at Loki who was tugging at his sleeve in a bid to lead him out of the hall.

"Thor, it has never been said that there is poor hospitality in Utgard," said Utgard-Loki quietly. "Show us how brave you really are by staying out your defeat and taking food and drink with us. Tomorrow I shall myself walk with you part of the way back to Asgard."

Thor struggled with his dignity but then swallowed his pride, what there was left of it, and he and Loki stayed in the great hall that night. They were made welcome and the food and wine were in plentiful supply, as were good companionship and laughter. No one referred to the competitions earlier in the day, and, when they lay down wrapped in huge bearskins in front of the fire for the night, Thor and Loki slept deeply and peacefully.

As the first light of dawn pierced through the smoke hole in the great hall, Thor and Loki awoke to find Utgard-Loki waiting for them. They walked out of the hall into the clear cold morning and made their way through the gates and out of the mighty walls. As they walked across the wide plain, Thor was unusually silent, his mind still returning uncomfortably to his humiliation of the previous day.

Then Utgard-Loki spoke. "I must leave you here, Thor. Now, I have to tell you that never again will you see inside the great walls of Utgard for as long as I live. If I had known just how fearsomely strong you were, I would have made very sure that you were never allowed anywhere near my giants in the first place," and he grimaced as though in pain.

Thor looked at Utgard-Loki in great bewilderment, but a knowing smile began to twitch at the corner of Loki's lips.

"I used trickery to defeat you in the competitions, Thor. You were dismayed that you were unable to empty the drinking horn, I was dismayed by how much you did manage to swallow! At the other end of the horn was the huge and mighty ocean. When you look at it next you will see that the shoreline has shifted many leagues out to sea. And that was no cat you lifted, it was Jormungand, the colossal coiled serpent that encircles the entire world, its tail in its mouth. Even to lift one paw off the ground was a terrifying feat. But most of all, Thor, I was frightened by how long you were able to withstand Elli, for Elli is Old Age and none can withstand Old Age. You may survive war and tempest and the sword, but Old Age will always win in the end."

Thor was white with rage. How dare Utgard-Loki use trickery to defeat and humiliate him in front of so many! He raised his mighty hammer in his huge hands and swung it back ready to deliver a final blow, but when he looked again, Utgard-Loki had disappeared as if he had never been there. Thor looked in every direction but of Utgard-Loki there was not a trace. Nor indeed could he see the gates and walls of Utgard.

"See," said Loki. "I told you that brains were needed to go to Utgard!" he said triumphantly.

Thor cuffed him around the ears yet again, and bent down very close, closing one huge fist around Loki's neck while glaring deep into his eyes. "If one

single word of this Utgard trickery ever leaves your lips, I shall know instantly and I will strike you such a blow with my hammer that you will soar right up into the heavens and never stop spinning even into deepest eternity. Do you mark my words well and understand, you snivelling tricky creature?" he whispered fiercely.

Loki did understand very well, and he spluttered his promise to Thor but he stored it all up in his cunning head with a quiet smile, and followed close on the heels of Thor as he strode back to Asgard, Thor once again filled with pride, for was he not indeed the mightiest of the gods?

The Old Man and the Beanstalk

The old man and his wife were at their wits' end. Their little field was full of stones and not much else. The carrots were all gone and the beanstalks were bare. All they had left was one small bag of beans, and before long that was empty, too. But not quite: just as the old man rolled the bag up to put it away in their big oak chest, something rolled out onto the floor.

"Wife, wife! I do believe there is something left in the old bean bag after all!" he called to the old woman who was searching the empty food safe just one more time in case she had missed a crust of bread or a rind of cheese. She came running at the sound of his voice, and together they knelt down on the hard floor to see just what had fallen from the bean bag.

"I can see something under here," said the old man and he stretched as far as he could under the chest. His scrabbling fingers closed around something and he pulled it out into the light. He opened his hand expectantly, and there lay … a bean.

"Pah!" snorted the old woman in disgust. "It is just an old bean," and she struggled to her feet, her eyes dull with disappointment.

But the old man was dancing with excitement. "Wife, wife, look! This is no ordinary bean," he laughed, "this is a special bean." And as she looked again, the old woman could see that he was right. The bean was twice the size as usual and it was a strange blue colour. The old man took the bean straight outside and planted it right in the middle of the stony little field. He watered it carefully and placed a tall stick alongside to support the plant when it appeared. That night, the old man and his wife went to bed with empty stomachs again, but as he closed his eyes the old man wished for a successful crop from the strange bean.

When they awoke in the morning, it was curiously dark. The old man and his wife struggled into their clothes in the half-light, wondering all the while at the green shadows that were flitting across the rough stone walls of the cottage. When they opened the door, a wondrous sight greeted them. As far as the eye could see, and beyond, a huge sturdy beanstalk reached up into the sky. The topmost leaves were lost in the clouds and the whole thing swayed in the wind.

"Gracious me!" exclaimed the old man. "I wished for a successful crop from our strange bean, but this is amazing."

But the old woman's eyes were full of mistrust. "There is something not right here, husband. First this great beanstalk has appeared as if by magic overnight," and here she lowered her voice for she had a great fear of all things magic, "and then if you look closely, husband, you will see that this beanstalk bears not one single bean!"

And she was right. When the old man stood at the foot of the huge beanstalk he could see that there was indeed not a bean to be seen. "Well, this is passing strange," he murmured and he scratched his head in bewilderment. The old couple went back indoors. But the old man could not settle. He kept coming out again to look at the massive beanstalk, its uttermost top leaves wreathed in clouds. "Perhaps I should just climb a little way up to see what I can see?" the old man asked, but the old woman thought this was a dreadful idea.

"Certainly not, husband! Have you taken leave of your senses? Aside from the foolishness of your thinking you are able to climb beanstalks at your age, there is the question of just what lies at the top of this particular beanstalk," answered the old woman crossly.

"But that is the point," said the old man mildly. "Just what does lie at the top?" And he simply could not get this thought out of his mind. He walked around the bottom of the beanstalk several times. He looked high up into the sky until his neck ached. Then he walked around the bottom again, and while he was around the far side he resolved to explore further. So with surprising agility (for he was a very old man) he started to climb up the beanstalk. The very second she realized what he was up to, the old woman whirled around the foot of the beanstalk with surprising agility (for she was a very old woman) and tried to grab the old man's shirt-tail. But she just could not reach.

"Husband, husband! You are too old for such behavior. What will happen to me if you fall and break your neck?" she yelled after him, but in vain.

Up and up he climbed steadily, pausing now and again to get his breath, the old woman still shouting imprecations from the ground. After a while, he could no longer hear her voice and so he just doggedly climbed and climbed up through the clouds. But then he began to hear more angry voices. He realized with a sinking heart that his wife was probably right to be afraid of what might happen to him. At that moment, his head broke through the clouds and he saw two things at once. Firstly, he had reached the very top of the beanstalk, and secondly, before him stood two simply enormous giants.

One was old and bent with long gray hair and a straggling beard, and he wore a robe of the palest blue with a wreath of ivy leaves around his head. The other was young and had corn-colored hair down to his waist. He wore a long jerkin of pure white lamb's wool and a ring of brightly colored flowers encircled his hair. The two were shouting at each other, and the breath of the old giant was as chill as the ice while the young giant's was warm and balmy. As soon as they saw the old man, they stopped mid-shout and peered down at him.

"Well, well, what have we here?" asked the young giant.

The old man was somewhat out of breath after his climb, but he managed to splutter out his apologies before explaining about the magical bean.

"As you are here, you can help us resolve our dispute," said the old giant gruffly. "I am Winter, he is Summer. Tell us now, little man, who is the most important?"

The old man realized his answer might be rather crucial to his future wellbeing, so he thought long and hard before answering the two huge giants. "I have to tell you that you are both important," he said finally.

This was not the answer the giants had been looking for, and they both stepped forward, frowning.

"You are both important," said the old man hastily, "because Summer makes the crops ripen and so we all have food to eat, but the earth needs to rest after the harvest so Winter gives everyone time to sleep."

The giants nodded and then smiled at the old man. "Well said, old man! You are wiser than one might think of someone who has just climbed up a strange beanstalk," laughed Summer. And Winter bent down and placed a simple earthenware pot at the old man's feet.

"This pot is our gift to you. Ask it for whatever you want, and you shall have all you ever need for the rest of your days. But tell no one about the pot other than your wife. Now be off, you have settled our dispute, and your poor wife is in despair down on the ground," said Winter.

So the old man thanked the giants for their great kindness, and began the long, slow descent back to his stony field, the earthenware pot clasped firmly in his arms. Down and down he went, sometimes slipping in his haste, and constantly fearful of breaking the pot. As he slithered the last few feet to the ground, the old woman rushed up and flung her arms around him in relief for, despite her scolding, she loved him dearly.

After a somewhat tearful reunion, the old man said, "Now, wife, I have a great treasure here; we will never want for anything for the rest of our days."

Of course the old woman thought he had taken leave of his senses, but she watched as he put the pot down carefully on their bare scrubbed table.

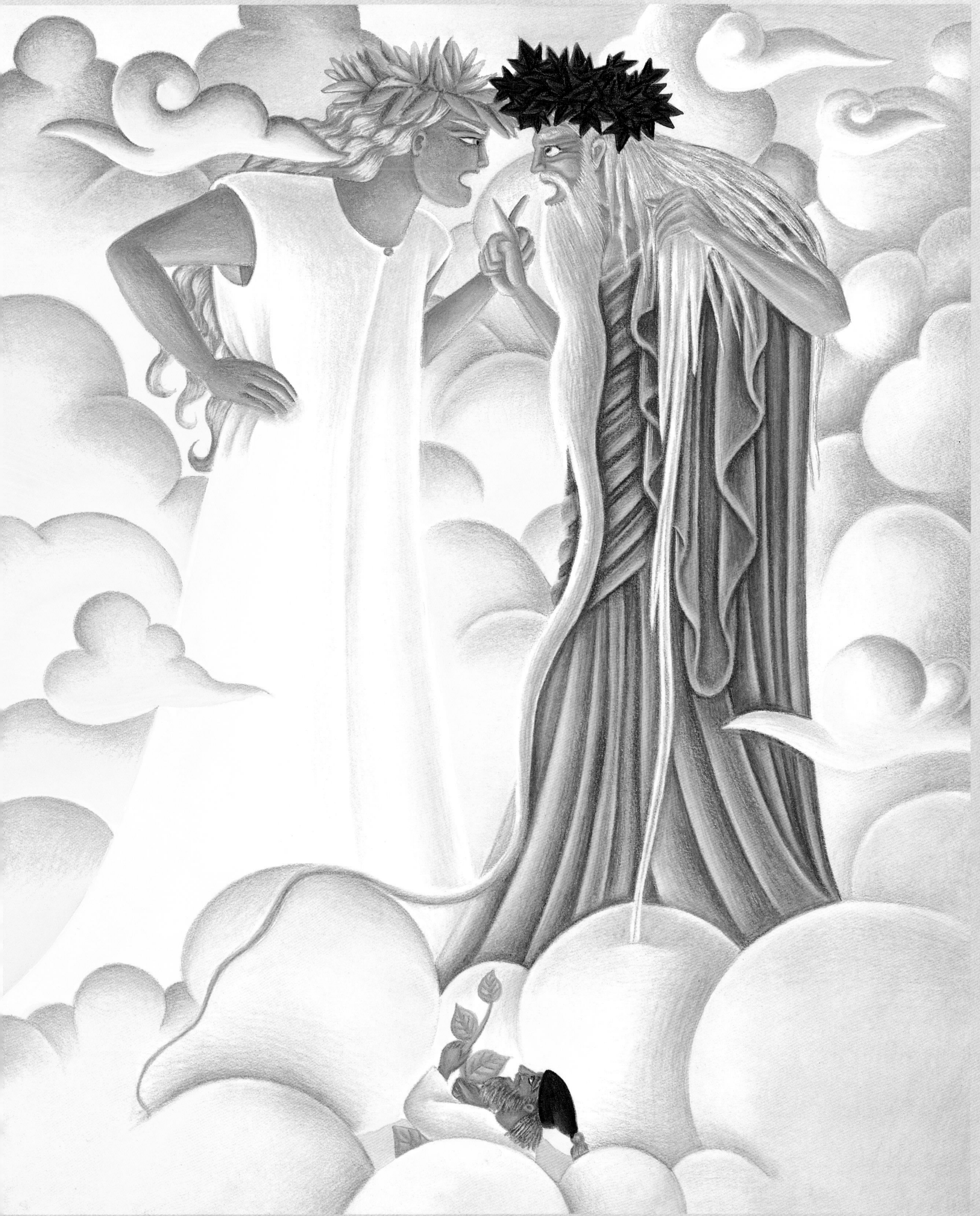

"If you please, pot, my wife and I are very hungry. Please may we have something to eat for breakfast?" the old man said and stood back expectantly. Well, his wife was just about to say "Stuff and nonsense!" when a brightly colored cloth whirled onto the table, and was soon covered with a wide bowl of fresh yogurt, a glistening honeycomb, a huge platter of fresh fruit and a crusty loaf of bread. A dish of deep yellow butter and a round goat's cheese completed the feast. The old man and the old woman were stunned into utter silence, but soon the wonderful smell of the bread roused them and they set to with a will, eating the first good meal they had enjoyed in years.

As you can imagine, the old man and the old woman then lived in great contentment for many a day to come, never lacking in food, or warm clothes for the bitter winter, or seeds to plant in the ground in the spring, for the simple earthenware pot never let them down. The giant beanstalk didn't grow any more, but neither did it produce any beans. All might have been well with the old couple had their son not returned unexpectedly one day.

He had been away for more years than any of them cared to remember, serving the king as a soldier in a far-off and inhospitable land. Of course, they were delighted to see him again and the pot provided a rare feast that night to celebrate his return. But the old woman could see that her son was deeply unhappy despite being home at last, and it did not take her long to prise out of the young man that he had fallen head-over-heels in love with the king's daughter. Now, a more sensible mother would have laughed and ruffled the son's hair and told him that was impossible and anyway there were plenty more fish in the sea, but the old woman had become rather used to having whatever she wanted with the magic pot. So she just tucked the pot under her arm, told the young man sharply to stop dawdling, and strode out of the door in the direction of the palace.

Now the son was a handsome enough fellow and he had a kind heart, but when the old woman arrived at the palace and demanded to speak to the king because her son had fallen in love with the princess, the king's reply was stern.

"I can see no sign that your son, handsome though he is, could provide for my daughter who, after all, is used to only the best. Let him build my daughter a palace of gold and silver, and let the palace be set in a gorgeous garden brimming with perfumed flowers from all around the world and filled with rare hummingbirds. Then I will consider the matter again," and of course the king thought that was the end of the matter. The princess thought so too, rather sorrowfully, for beyond his good looks, she had perceived that here was a kindly man she might be very happy to marry.

But, of course, the simple matter of a palace of gold and silver set in a gorgeous garden brimming with perfumed flowers from all around the world and filled with rare hummingbirds was no difficulty for the pot. In the morning, when the king and the queen woke up, their bedchamber was filled with a bright light, and when the footman drew back the heavy brocade curtains, there was the gleaming palace and the gardens and the perfumed flowers and the rare hummingbirds.

"I smell magic," said the queen. "We need to find out how that simple old woman was able to make this happen." And so the old woman was summoned, together with the old man and, of course, the son came along as well. Quite who revealed the secret of the pot would be hard to say, but revealed it was, and I am sorry to say that the king and the queen arranged for the pot to be stolen, and another similar pot to be left in its place, that very night from the poor cottage where the old couple lived. This was a particularly mean thing to do, and certainly not at all honourable, and hardly the behavior you might expect from a king and queen. But there it is. When the old couple asked the pot for breakfast the following morning, absolutely nothing happened, and they realized they had been tricked.

They were much too afraid to do anything about it: after all, it is a little difficult to accuse the king and queen of stealing. The old woman was sad because her son was sad, and the old man was sad because they were sad. The princess was sad and cross too, because she thought her parents had behaved very badly, but she too was afraid to do anything about it for it is just as hard for a princess to accuse the king and queen of stealing.

The old man had grown used to having good meals every day and so before too long he was very hungry indeed. He resolved to climb the beanstalk once more and to seek out Summer and Winter to ask them what they would do.

So up and up he climbed, even more slowly this time as he had become rather stout with all the good meals, but he eventually puffed to the top of the beanstalk. He looked all around and then he felt a breeze, cool on one side of his face and warm on the other, and there in front of him stood the two giants.

Winter looked sadly at the old man. "Well, well, little man, why have you returned to us?" he said.

The old man did not answer. Suddenly he felt ashamed of his errand.

Summer laughed, and his laugh filled the air it was so big and warm. "Have you lost the pot?" he asked.

The old man nodded sadly. And then he told the giants the whole story.

They listened carefully and when the old man had finished they smiled at him again.

"We did tell you not to tell anyone," Summer rumbled. "Now you know why."

"But we have been able to live in great harmony since you last visited us, thanks to your wisdom," said Winter, "and so we will give you another gift. Use it wisely and you may have restored to you what is rightly yours."

"And your son may yet marry his princess!" laughed Summer, and his warm breath cheered the old man.

The giants presented him with an old gnarled stick. "Just say to it 'Give me what I deserve' and the stick will do the rest," and with that the giants waved the old man off down the beanstalk again.

As soon as he reached the bottom, the old man rushed indoors and, expecting a good meal, he said to the stick, "Give me what I deserve," but instead of a delicious meal appearing, the stick began to beat the old man about the shoulders. "Stop! Stop!" he cried in pain, and the stick stopped right away. Then the old man understood. He grasped the stick firmly in his hand and said, "Give what is deserved to the thief who stole my pot," and in the twinkling of an eye the stick disappeared out of the door, and down the road in the direction of the palace.

Time passed, and then the old man and woman heard a commotion in the distance. Before much longer, they saw the king and the queen running down the road, the king roaring in pain, and the queen crying her eyes out. The stick was in hot pursuit, whacking the king and then the queen about the shoulders. Alongside ran the footman, the pot clasped tightly in his arms. The old man and the old woman laughed as much as they dared, but did not call off the stick until the pot stood on their scrubbed table once more.

The king and the queen sat down with a flump and then both began talking at once: "Can't tell you how ashamed—"

"—and of course your son—"

"—must marry the princess—"

"—as soon as possible!" they both said in a great rush which, of course, was just what everyone wanted to hear.

And so the young man married his princess and they lived happily ever after. The old man and the old woman never wanted for anything more ever again now that they had the pot back, so they lived happily ever after, too. The king and the queen went back to the palace after the wedding and the king used the stick to keep law and order in the country, and aside from the odd prick of conscience when they remembered how badly they had behaved, they lived happily ever after, too.

And what of the beanstalk? It just disappeared overnight, leaving not a trace behind. Not a leaf, not a branch and certainly not a single bean. So I can't tell you about the two giants, but if you listen very carefully you can hear them laughing sometimes, so I am sure they lived happily ever after, too!

Soliday and the Giant Man Crow

Deep in the lush jungle, where delicate waxy orchids grew and parrots swooped, there lived a huge and sinister bird. Man Crow was no ordinary bird: he was a giant. He had the body of a colossal human with great long arms ending in cruel talons, and huge strong legs, knotted with muscles. His glossy black head was that of a crow, and his small mean eyes missed nothing. His vicious beak snapped shut on golden teeth and a darting golden tongue. Sprouting from his massive shoulders were two immense wings, their glossy black feathers like an all-enveloping cloak. When Man Crow flew, darkness fell over all the land and fear gripped every heart. The tiny animals on the jungle floor cowered under the dripping leaves of the mangrove tree, and even the bigger animals stopped eating and looked for shelter. The hummingbirds darted into their mossy hanging nests and the trembling butterflies folded their wings. In the village, babies would cry out and reach for their mothers, and the men would reach for their bows and arrows. Man Crow gave a loud raucous "Caw!" and only flapped his horrid wings more so that the darkness was filled with a mighty rushing wind as well.

Time came when the people could no longer bear their fears, so they went to the headman of the village. He shook his head sadly and said, "People of mine, there is only one solution. Somehow, we must kill this wicked Man Crow. I will give the successful hunter my handsome daughter in marriage." Now this was a good reward, for the daughter she was a very fine woman. She could cook a good stew and she had a sweet husky voice when singing as she stirred the pot. So, many brave men tried their luck. They found Man Crow—he was not difficult to spot—but he only laughed at their futile efforts and swooped down on their heads, scattering them in terror.

In a far-off village there was a bright lad called Soliday. He lived with his grandmother and was a happy-go-lucky young man. One day, Soliday and his grandmother woke up early to find it was strangely dark and the banana trees were swaying as if in a great tempest. Soliday's grandmother crouched under her chair, her eyes closed tightly and her trembling hands clasped close together.

"What is it, Granny mine?" asked Soliday. "Why are you hiding, and why are the banana trees swaying?"

"Foolish boy! Why am I hiding? I am hiding because Man Crow is on the wing. He has spread this darkness over the land," she screeched.

Now Soliday had heard about Man Crow but the wicked bird had never flown this far before, so Soliday rushed outside to have a look at him. He came back in again very quickly. "He is very big, Granny, and he has snatched up some of our bananas in his talons!" yelled Soliday. And his granny began to cry. Now this made Soliday very angry, so, once the darkness had passed and he judged it safe to go outside again, he gathered together a few things and told his granny he would be out for a while. "You watch out for that Man Crow, Soliday!" she called after him, but he was well down the road.

Now Soliday was very afraid of Man Crow, but he didn't like to see his granny upset, and he was just mad at Man Crow for stealing their bananas, so he resolved to do something about the matter. On his back he slung his bow, and in his hand he carried six arrows. He was determined to succeed in despatching Man Crow where so many others before him had failed. "See if I don't kill that old Man Crow!" he chanted as he walked along the dusty track.

Soliday walked boldly into the jungle and soon all the parrots were chattering. "Soliday is coming! You better look out now, Man Crow!" But of Man Crow there was no sign. Soliday walked on and on, and the parrots soon fell silent. All Soliday could hear was the drip, drip, drip of water falling off the leaves. It grew darker and Soliday's knees began to tremble for he knew this was not just the darkness of the jungle. Man Crow must be near.

A harsh voice suddenly croaked, "Good day to you, Soliday, good day." Soliday's hair stood on end, and his heart somersaulted in his chest. It was Man Crow! Soliday peered up into the topmost branches of the trees, and there he saw the terrible gleaming feathered head with its vicious beak and as Man Crow spoke, Soliday caught a flash of the golden teeth and darting golden tongue.

"G-g-g-good day to you, Man Crow, too," stammered Soliday.

And Man Crow hopped down a branch to look at this impudent person who was apparently not too afraid to reply to him. Fortunately, he could not hear Soliday's teeth chattering. Soliday pulled his bow off his shoulders and strung one of his arrows, then aimed it at Man Crow. It missed, but two of Man Crow's black feathers fell to the ground. Man Crow flicked his golden tongue and flapped down another branch. "Hoo, hoo, Soliday. You are not trying to hit me, are you? I am much too clever for you to catch me unawares," he said harshly. Soliday let another arrow fly. Two more black feathers fell into his outstretched hand. Man Crow frowned and stumped down another branch.

Now all the while this was going on, another figure was watching, well hidden and silent. It was Anancy, the spider. Now, that Anancy, what a rogue and deceiver he was! He would lie and bluster his way out of any situation, and he was idle as a sloth and always ready to take credit for the good deeds of others. He was most interested in the headman's

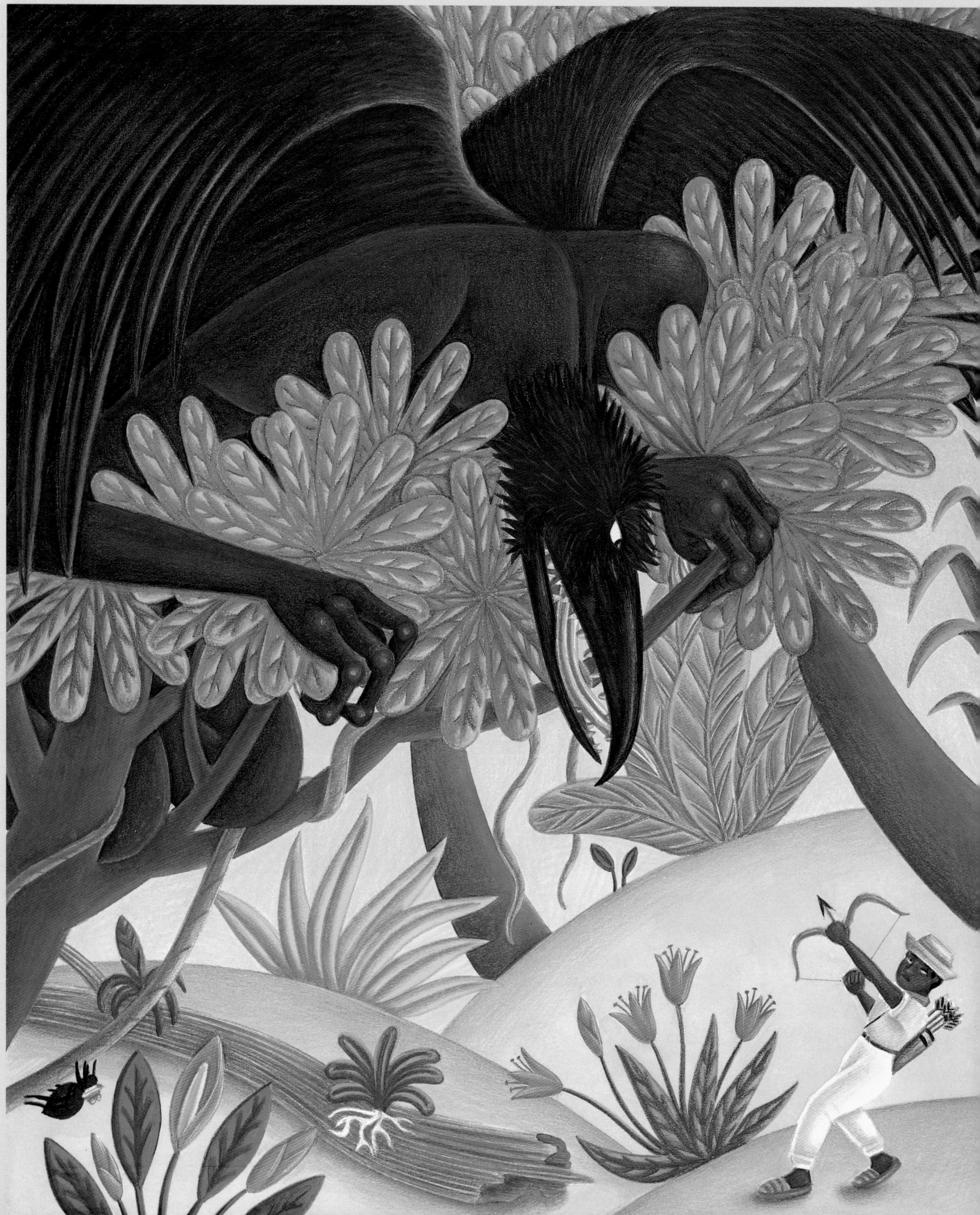

handsome daughter, but of course much too cowardly to try to deal with Man Crow himself.

Soliday sent another arrow up into the tree. Man Crow cawed in annoyance as two more glossy black feathers drifted down, and he jumped down another branch. Now Soliday could see just how immense Man Crow was, what use was a puny arrow? But he quickly strung another and up it flew high into the leaves. Man Crow had to pull his head up sharply as the arrow whizzed by hard into the tree. Two black feathers floated down.

"Soliday, you are really beginning to irritate me," shouted Man Crow, hopping down the tree again, but even before his talons had wrapped themselves around the branch, Soliday had sent up another arrow. It whistled through the feathers on the top of Man Crow's head. Man Crow let out a horrid yell, and when he looked, Soliday could see his small mean eyes were glittering with rage and malice.

But Soliday only had one arrow left so he knew this one had to fly true. He strung it very carefully and squinted up into the tree. Man Crow looked immense and he looked very angry. He spread his wings out and everything grew inky black. Soliday could only shoot blind, but he had not moved a muscle so up sang the arrow, clean into Man Crow's wicked heart. With one terrible great shriek of rage, Man Crow tumbled down through the branches to fall in a gigantic heap of feathers at Soliday's feet. He was quite dead. Soliday sank to his knees, his arms shaking from the tension of the bow, his heart beating as fast as a cricket. And all the while Anancy watched silently.

Soliday struggled to his feet. He skirted the great body until he came to the head. He clambered up over the smooth feathers and reaching inside the vast gaping beak, he cut out Man Crow's golden tongue. He wrapped it carefully in a huge vine leaf and put it in his bag together with the eight glossy black feathers, then he set off home to tell his grandmother she did not need to fear Man Crow anymore.

Anancy slid from his hiding place and, with his trickster's strength, he dragged Man Crow's great body to the headman. "Ho there!" he shouted. "It's me, Anancy. I have killed Man Crow!"

Everyone came flocking out and there right enough was Man Crow's huge body, and he was surely very dead. As people crowded around, Anancy's boasting grew ever more fanciful until the headman shouted for silence. "Anancy, how exactly did you kill Man Crow?" he asked sternly. Anancy drew in a deep breath and was about to embark on another fabulous string of lies when

Soliday and his grandmother appeared at the edge of the throng of people.

Soliday was carrying the feathers and the huge vine leaf with Man Crow's golden tongue. "Ah, I see that somehow you have the body of Man Crow," said Soliday. "I killed him," he continued proudly.

"That can't be," said the people. "Anancy brought the body here. He killed him."

Soliday held out the eight glossy black feathers and then opened the vine leaf and there was Man Crow's golden tongue. The headman peered inside Man Crow's beak and sure enough the tongue was missing.

"Anancy!" he roared, but Anancy was no longer to be found. As soon as he had seen Soliday coming, he had crept swiftly away from the great hubbub of people, and he was not seen in that particular village again for a very long time. Soliday was very pleased indeed to be married to the headman's handsome daughter and the wedding celebrations lasted for several days and nights.

Soliday and his bride together looked after his grandmother for many a long year to come. As for Man Crow, he passed into legend. Over the years, parents came to use the threat of a visit from him to get their children to behave, "That old Man Crow, he just waiting outside for you!"

And what of Anancy? Well, he was a trickster after all, so it was not too long before he was to be seen skulking around the jungle again, looking for more mischief. And he found it in the shape of a magic pot—but that is a story for another time!

The Giant of St. Michael's Mount

A very long time ago, an exceptionally large giant decided to set up home near the village of Marazion in Cornwall. The villagers quickly discovered that it was less than ideal having a giant as a neighbor. As he stomped about the place, his huge feet trampled on their potatoes, and, when he sat down, everyone had to scatter fast lest they be squashed.

Everyone thought he was rather hard of hearing, but in fact the truth was that his head was so high up in the clouds that human voices didn't carry that far. So he couldn't hear the villagers when they yelled at him to watch where he was walking, and thus he was unaware of the havoc he was causing. A time came when the villagers of Marazion felt they had had enough. So they all met one night when the giant was safely asleep in Hollow Tree Field, although his snoring was enough to make old Granny Pascoe—who was a bit hard of hearing herself—think that there was thunder in the air.

"What are we going to do about this giant, then?" asked Nelson Trethewy who was a fisherman. "Every time he paddles along the beach my boat gets swamped."

"And when he sneezes he blows the cows right out of the fields," said Sukey Chenoweth whose father was a farmer.

"My missus is fed up with his mucky footprints all over her garden," added Petroc Griglans.

"We need to get rid of him, that's what we need to do," said Jago Pengelly pompously, for he fancied himself to be the cleverest person in the whole of Marazion.

"Well of course we need to get rid of him, Jago Pengelly, we all know that!" said Nelson sharply. "But how are we going to do it?"

Because everyone was rather frightened of the giant, but anxious at the same time not to upset him unnecessarily (for goodness knows what might happen then) there was a lot of heated talking and cross muttering, but they were getting nowhere when a quiet voice said, "I have an idea."

It was Landon Penwether, a young farmer who lived with his widowed mother just outside the village. He kept himself to himself, only coming in to Marazion for a few provisions once a month, but everyone knew him to be hardworking and to have the straightest furrows and the finest herd of cattle for many a mile.

"What are we Cornish men famed for?" he asked.

"Fishing," called out Nelson.

"Farming," shouted Zach Tregeagle from Tamarisk Farm.

"Clotted cream," blurted out Jago, and everyone glared at him for being so frivolous during such a serious discussion.

"All of those and more," said Landon, "but what I am thinking of is mining."

Everyone looked around. There was no doubt about their skills as miners, but what ever did that have to do with getting rid of a troublesome giant?

"What we need to do," began Landon patiently, "is to tunnel into the hillside, so we can dig out a deep pit underneath the ground. From above, the grass will grow and the flowers bloom as before and it will look like firm land. But when the giant comes along, as soon as he stands on it, his great weight will make the covering collapse and he will fall into the pit, bringing his head onto a level where we can converse. We can explain very politely what he is doing to our village and ask him to be more careful in future."

Landon had not said so much at one go in all the years he had lived in Marazion, so he sat down quickly after this with rather a bump. There was a stunned silence and then everyone

began talking at once. It seemed like a good idea, but who was going to talk to the giant once he was in the pit, for to be sure he would not be in an amiable frame of mind! Everyone looked around the room, not daring to meet another's eye lest that be seen as volunteering for this dangerous task.

But Landon had thought of that. "I will get my mother to talk to the giant," he said presently. "She will know what to say."

And so it was that the villagers of Marazion began the task of catching their giant. A troop of men gathered together, all carrying shovels and pickaxes, and they crept under cover of darkness to the place Landon had selected. They tunnelled silently and dug endlessly through the night for a week, and at the end of that time there was a huge pile of rocks and stones and earth where before there was a field full of cows. There was also a very fragile layer of earth left over the top of a deep pit that the miners had dug out. All they needed to do now was wait for the giant.

Landon had chosen the spot well for it lay directly on the way to the beach and, as Nelson knew to his cost, the giant was very fond of paddling in the sea. On the morning of the second day after the pit was ready, the giant came thump, thumping down towards the sea. It was a beautiful morning. The early sun glinted on the calm grey sea, the skylarks were high in the sky and the giant hummed to himself tunelessly as he made his destructive way to the beach. Mrs. Griglans' sweetpeas were crushed under one foot while Sukey Chenoweth watched in dismay as the giant's other foot trailed all her newly pegged out washing through the mud in the farmyard. The giant didn't notice the huge pile of rocks and stones and earth. He didn't see the little gaggle of miners hidden by the hillside. He just trampled through the hedges and then there was a great whoosh and the giant gave an almighty yell as he fell down, down into the deep pit, right up to his neck. And there he was stuck.

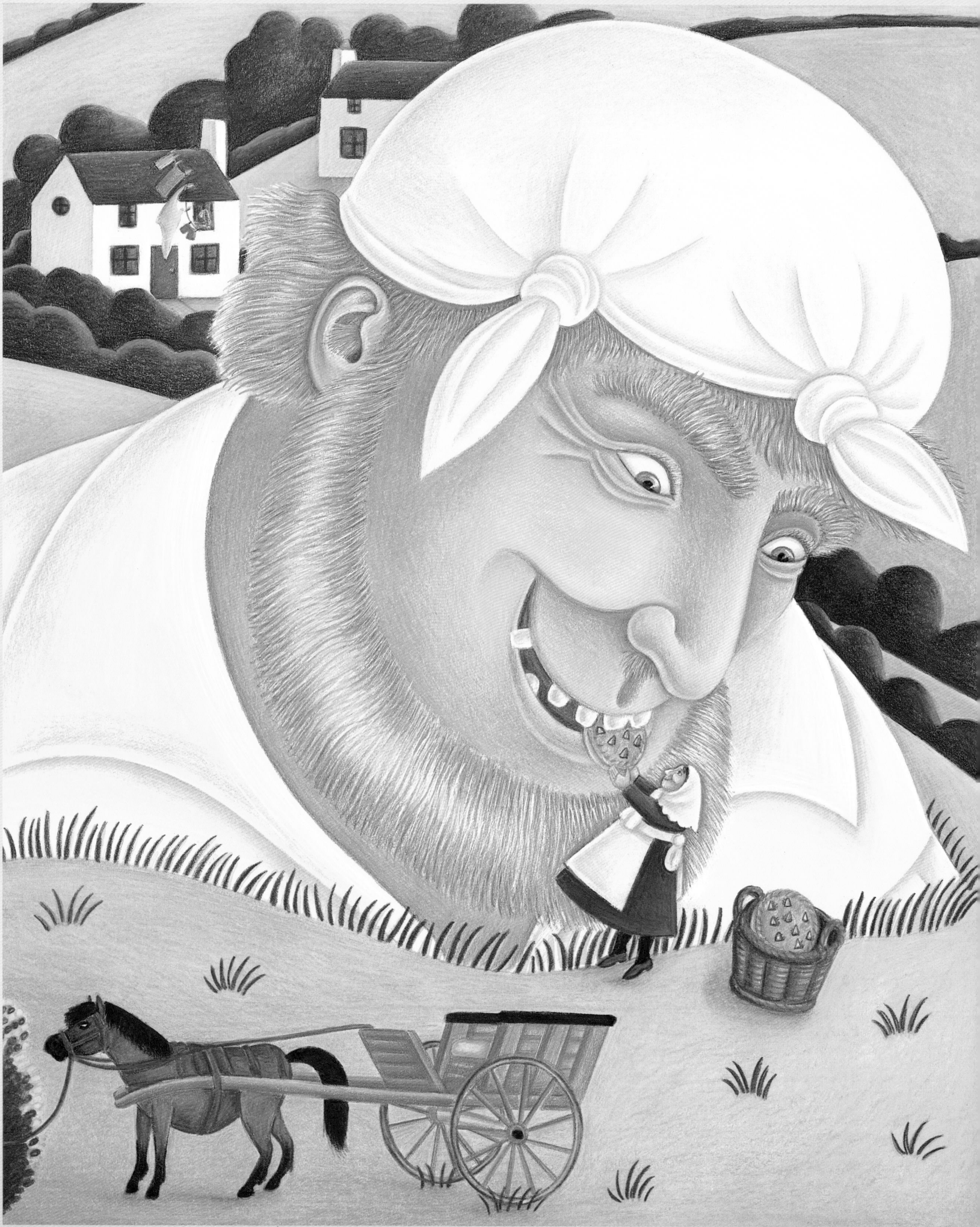

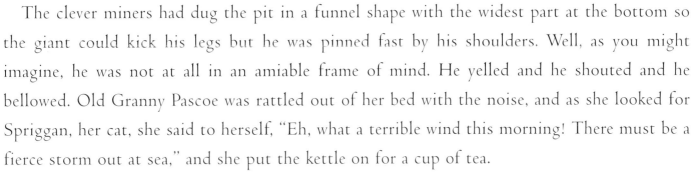

The clever miners had dug the pit in a funnel shape with the widest part at the bottom so the giant could kick his legs but he was pinned fast by his shoulders. Well, as you might imagine, he was not at all in an amiable frame of mind. He yelled and he shouted and he bellowed. Old Granny Pascoe was rattled out of her bed with the noise, and as she looked for Spriggan, her cat, she said to herself, "Eh, what a terrible wind this morning! There must be a fierce storm out at sea," and she put the kettle on for a cup of tea.

At the same moment a neat cart trundled over the hill, a sturdy pit pony in the shafts. Landon's mother, Mrs. Penwether, sat in the cart, a big wicker basket at her feet. She guided the pony down towards the giant's bellowing head and tethered the cart to a nearby gorse bush. Then she picked up the big wicker basket and made her way closer to the angry giant. There was a delicious smell rising from the basket.

Close up, the giant was a sorry sight. His very blue eyes appeared to be filled with tears and his huge mouth turned down at the corners.

"Now then," said Mrs. Penwether, "do stop making that dreadful noise. You are giving me a headache. My son, Landon, will see to it that you are set free very soon. You and I need to have a little talk. But I imagine you are hungry, would you like a piece of my stargazy pie first of all?"

The giant stopped shouting and looked carefully at the tiny bustling lady who had appeared just under his chin. He gave a great sniff and as he did so, the most wonderful smell filled his nostrils. The tiny lady was holding up something in both her hands. It was a huge pie, a stargazy pie. Now stargazy pie is made with pilchards which are cooked whole with their heads all popping through the crust. It is very delicious and it was the giant's favourite, but no one had made it for him since he was a young giantling. He licked his lips, stretched out his neck and then, very carefully and with considerable delicacy for such a big person, he took the pie between his teeth and began to eat. "Mmmmm!" he boomed. "Thank you very much, that was delicious."

"There is no need to shout, dear," said Mrs. Penwether, handing up another stargazy pie to the appreciative giant.

The second pie disappeared as fast as the first but this time the giant did his best to whisper as he said, "Thank you. I have not tasted such a good stargazy pie in all my life," and his great face was wreathed in smiles.

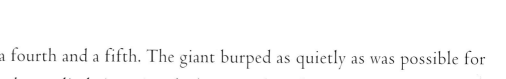
A third pie followed and a fourth and a fifth. The giant burped as quietly as was possible for a giant, and then Mrs. Penwether, politely ignoring the burp, said to the giant, "Now look here, young man—what is your name, by the way?"

"Michael," said the giant.

"Well, Michael, the thing is, you are such a great big fellow that you are causing great damage wherever you go. You put your feet into gardens and farmyards, you frighten the animals and your snoring keeps us awake at night."

The giant hung his huge head in shame. "I had no idea," he said. "Why didn't anyone tell me?"

"Ah well, there you have it," said Mrs. Penwether. "Your head is so far up in the clouds that we could never get you to hear us, and that is why we dug this hole, so you and I could talk on a level, so to speak," and she passed the giant yet another stargazy pie.

As the giant munched, Mrs. Penwether patiently explained that while the people of Marazion were proud and privileged to have a giant in their midst, something needed to be done. Michael could see this. He was, in fact, a very gentle creature, fond of children and liking nothing better than walking in the countryside and splashing through the waves—and stargazy pie, of course.

Suddenly Michael's face lit up. He was looking at the huge pile of rocks and stones and earth. "I have an idea! Why don't I transport all those rocks and stones into the sea and make myself an island where I can live on my own without harming anyone and yet I'll still be able to see and visit everyone in Marazion! If I came when you were expecting me, you could show me where it was safe for me to walk," Michael said happily.

Mrs. Penwether was delighted. She clapped her hands and said, "There now, Michael, that is a splendid idea. We shall all help you move the rocks and stones," and she called to the hidden miners, and, as they emerged from their

hiding place, she told them the wonderful solution to the problem.

The miners worked without pause to release Michael who then sat down, very carefully indeed, and they all discussed the best way to transport the rocks and stones down to the seashore. Michael said he could then carry it all in his huge arms through the waves to a suitable point off the coast. And so it happened. The very next day was like a huge party. Everyone in Marazion came out to help and to encourage or just to watch as the miners and Michael carried every last rock and stone from the pit down to the seashore. All day long, an impressive island took shape off the coastline, and by the time the sun was setting, there was the giant sitting in great happiness on his very own island. That night everyone slept well, the villagers secure in the knowledge that their animals and crops were safe, and the giant happy in his new home.

The following morning, just as the sun was rising, the giant looked out towards Marazion. The tide was out and a neat cart came trundling across the sand causeway, a sturdy pit pony in the shafts. Holding the reins was Landon Penwether, his mother by his side holding a very large wicker basket on her lap. Michael scrambled to his feet and went down his island to the sands to wait for the cart.

"Good morning, Michael," called Mrs. Penwether cheerfully.

Landon stepped onto the rocks and carefully handed his mother out of the cart and then lifted down the wicker basket. There was a delicious smell rising from the basket. Landon shouted up to the giant. "All the men of Marazion are ready to come and help you build a castle to keep you warm and dry in the winter," and Michael could see that already a great stream of men, all carrying shovels and pickaxes, were pouring across the causeway.

"Thank you!" he whispered, for he had remembered what Mrs. Penwether had said about his great booming voice.

"And I have brought you something too," smiled Mrs. Penwether, opening the basket. It was full of stargazy pies!

So everyone lived happily ever after. Michael settled into his splendid new castle (you can still see it there today) and the villagers of Marazion became very proud of their own giant. Landon married Sukey Chenoweth and they had lots of children who used to visit Michael often. They would all climb up onto his huge lap, and he would tell them stories of the old giants of Cornwall. And every week, Mrs. Penwether would bake a huge batch of stargazy pies, especially for the giant of St. Michael's Mount.

A Tale of the Tsarevna and the Seven Giants

The tsar had gone on a long journey, leaving the tsarina behind in the great cold and glittering palace. She was expecting their first child, so she was particularly sad to see the tsar's cavalcade of horses disappear over the snowy steppe. From that moment on, she sat every day at her window, gazing over the white landscape, but of the returning tsar there was no sign. Every day she watched and waited, but all she saw was swirling snow as the drifts grew ever deeper.

Nine long months passed. Then, on Christmas Eve, the tsarina gave birth to a tiny daughter. Just as midnight was striking, and with the wind howling around his head, the tsar strode in through the palace, stamping his great boots and shaking the snow off his huge wolfskin cape as he rushed upstairs to the room where his tsarina and their new baby daughter lay together wrapped warmly in rugs by a blazing log fire. The tsarina gave the tsar one sad smile and then closed her eyes, never to open them again. The birth of her daughter and the strain of waiting for the tsar to return had used all her strength, and she died that morning.

The tsar was heartbroken. For months he wandered through the palace aimlessly, seemingly oblivious to all that went on around him. Meanwhile, his tiny daughter, the tsarevna, enchanted all who met her. Ever smiling, she had the fairest hair and deep blue eyes and her skin was as white as the snow that her mother had gazed out on for all those months.

A year passed and the tsar was persuaded to take a new wife. She was tall and very beautiful, with long black hair that she wore in two great braids that fell past her waist. Her eyes were deep green and she always wore black velvet robes with silver braiding and silver fox fur around the neck and cuffs. A silver crown glittered on her head and on her feet she wore silver boots. She looked every inch a tsarina, but her heart was as cold as the icy steppe. She was proud and vain, and she hated the tiny tsarevna.

In amongst her many trunks of clothes and perfumes and the like, the new tsarina had brought with her a very special mirror. Now this mirror could speak, and whenever the tsarina would look into it, which she did several times a day, she would ask it how beautiful she was, and the mirror would purr softly and say, "Your beauty is astounding, my lady. There is no one on earth who can compare with you," and other such ridiculously flattering things, all of which the tsarina would listen to with a greedy look in her green eyes and laughter in her throat. Then she was happy for a while.

Years passed and the tsarevna grew into a lovely young woman. Her father adored her and bought her beautiful, rich brocaded dresses and the softest woollen wraps made of the finest cashmere. He gave her rings of opals for her delicate white fingers and strings of rare river pearls to hang around her neck. And finally he arranged for her to be betrothed to Nikolai, the son of a fabulously wealthy merchant. Nikolai adored the tsarevna and she him, so plans were made for their wedding.

On the morning of the wedding, the tsarina asked the mirror her usual question, and the answer was not at all what she wanted to hear.

"Your beauty is still astounding, my lady, but the tsarevna is lovelier by far," and the mirror sniggered softly. The tsarina flung her hairbrush at the mirror in a huge temper, but still it said, "The tsarevna is lovelier by far."

The tsarina was beside herself. Never had the mirror denied her, and now it was her hated step-daughter who had usurped her. She called angrily for her servant-girl, Chernavka. When she appeared (looking fearfully down at the floor, so great was her mistress's rage) the tsarina hissed her instructions in a low whisper: "Get hold of the tsarevna and take her to the deepest, darkest part of the forest where you must leave her tied to a tree so she will be taken by the wolves."

Chernavka was horrified and this must have shown on her face.

"Do it, and do it now, or it will be the worse for you," snarled the tsarina, and she certainly did not look beautiful as she spoke, her face all contorted with rage. "If you fail me in this, I shall have you nailed up in a barrel and rolled off into the deepest snowdrift," the tsarina added.

With a heavy heart, Chernavka went in search of the tsarevna. She found her surrounded by her maids who were bustling around, fussing with the tsarevna's hair, buffing her nails and spraying clouds of perfume all over the room. Chernavka shooed them all away and then, gritting her teeth, she put on her widest smile and said, "I have such a wonderful surprise to show you! Your Nikolai has arranged it all as a special present for you and he is the only other person who knows what it is. You must come with me into the forest, come quickly now!" and she turned her head away for fear the tsarevna would see the lie in her eyes.

The tsarevna was concerned that such an expedition would make her late for her wedding, but Chernavka promised her that they would be back in time. She wrapped the tsarevna in the warmest furs and scarves, and pushed her feet into her thick boots, then she took her by the hand and led her far away from the palace and deep into the forest.

The tsarevna was at first excited and chattered gaily, then she became puzzled, but then she grew frightened, and as she began to cry she asked Chernavka where they were going. Before long, Chernavka was crying too and then she spilled out the whole terrible story to the tsarevna. The tsarevna could see nothing was to be gained by her tears, so she dried her eyes, shooed Chernavka back to the palace and determinedly set about walking as fast as she could in the opposite direction, as she now understood that the wicked tsarina would stop at nothing to ensure her beauty remained unchallenged.

Chernavka stumbled back to the palace and told the tsarina that she had taken the tsarevna into the forest and, crossing her fingers behind her back, suggested that even now she was probably being set upon by wolves.

The tsarina confronted the mirror. It simpered, "Your beauty is astounding, my lady."

So delighted was the tsarina that she did not notice the mirror appeared to hesitate after it spoke, as if there was something else it wanted to say.

The tsarina primped and preened for a while, and then joined the tsar in the pale blue and silver ballroom to celebrate the wedding of Nikolai and the tsarevna. But, of course, the tsarevna did not appear, and after an increasingly frantic search of the palace it was decided that she must have been kidnapped. Nikolai wasted no time in saddling up his big black horse and galloping off to seek out the old wise woman who lived in the nearest village. He felt sure she would give him guidance as he sought to track down the tsarevna, wherever she might have been taken.

The tsarevna, meanwhile, was tramping through the forest, anxious to find somewhere to shelter for the night. She thought she could hear wolves howling in the distance and she was growing very tired. But then she heard a dog barking, and it seemed quite near. "Where there is a dog, there must also be people," she said to herself, and she walked faster towards the sound. Suddenly she came across a clearing and there in front of her stood a house, quite ordinary in every aspect except its size. The windows were huge, the front door was huge, and the bench outside the door was huge. The dog, however, was small and very pleased to see her. It bounded up and licked her hand, then trotted in through the huge front door which lay slightly ajar. The dog looked over its shoulder and seemed to be encouraging her to come in, so the tsarevna followed cautiously behind.

Inside, everything was once again quite ordinary in every aspect except size. The table covered in dirty dishes was huge. Seven huge stools were scattered around and seven huge armchairs were ranged around the unlit stove. The dog danced at her feet and then seemed to invite the tsarevna to climb up the huge staircase where she found seven huge and unmade beds.

The tsarevna felt no fear; somehow it was a friendly house. She went back downstairs and set about tidying up. She straightened the huge stools around the table. She cleared the table and washed up the seven huge bowls and the seven huge goblets and the seven huge knives and forks, and then she piled the stove high with logs and soon had a warming fire going. She made the seven huge beds. She lit the candle in front of the icon just inside the huge door and then she and the little dog curled up together on the huge rug in front of the stove and both fell fast asleep.

From outside after a while came the sound of cheerful singing and the tramp of huge boots, and, as the door burst open, seven huge young giants tumbled inside. They made so much noise that both the dog and the tsarevna both awoke with a start. The dog rushed up to the huge young men, wagging his tail in delight. The tsarevna stood up and smoothed her crumpled dress and smiled nervously.

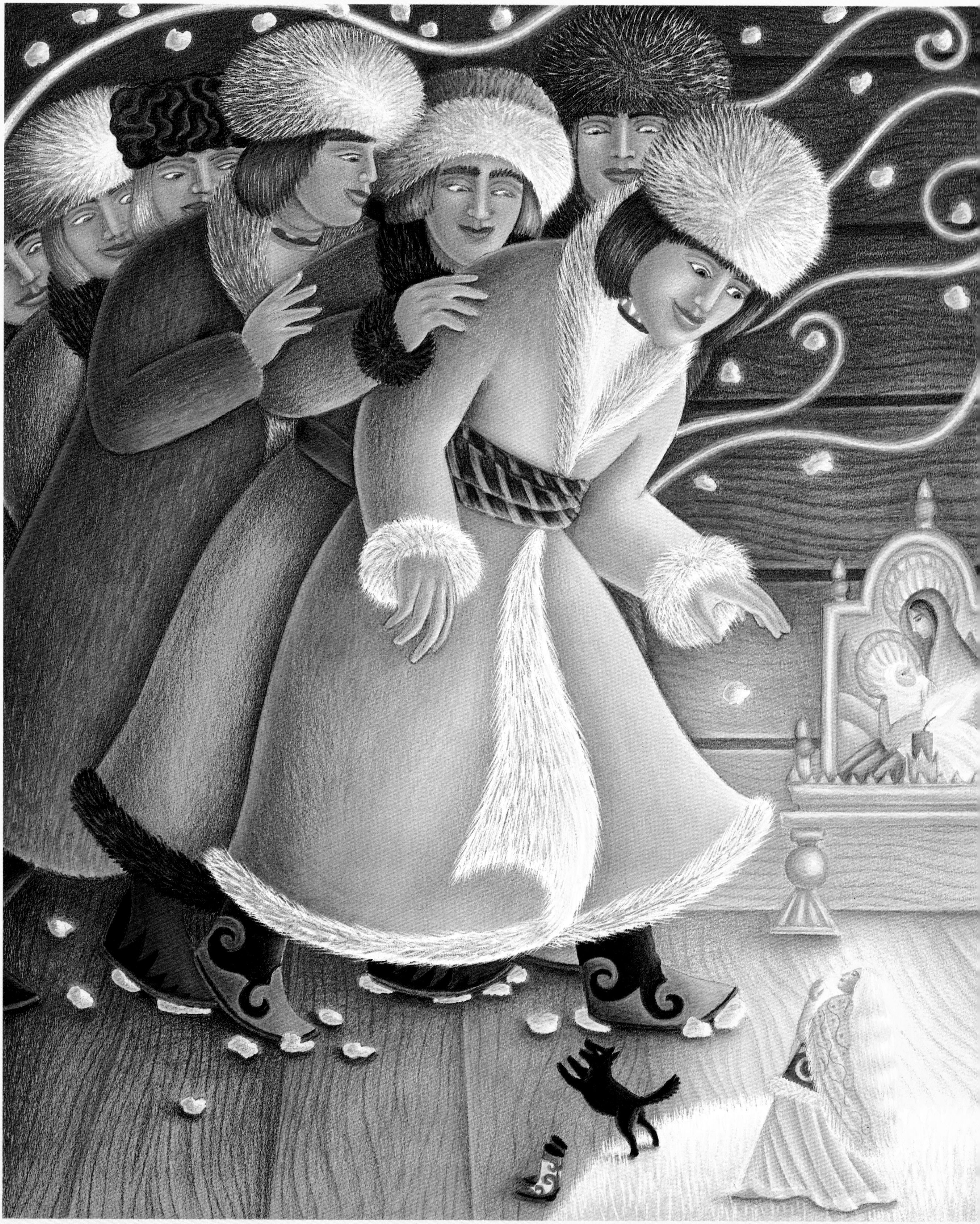

For a moment they all looked at each other in utter silence and then everyone started talking at once. The giants were delighted with their tidy house, and the tsarevna was delighted to find seven champions for, of course, they were very angry when they heard why the tsarevna had ended up in their home. Everyone rushed around and soon supper was on the table. The tsarevna could not be persuaded to drink any vodka but she did have a very, very small slice of the huge game pie that the giants set upon the table. After the meal, one of the giants—who were all brothers, the tsarevna learned—made a simple bed out of logs and furs and it was placed carefully behind the stove so that the tsarevna might have a cosy corner all of her own. As she lay in the dark, the little dog curled by her side and the soft glow from the candle in front of the icon to comfort her, the tsarevna smiled to herself for the first time in what had been a very dark day.

The next day, and the next, and the next after that, the seven giants and the tsarevna all settled down into a happy and comfortable routine. The giants would go out in the morning to patrol the forest. Sometimes they might meet a band of fierce Tartars and that night the tsarevna would have cuts and bruises to attend to, but mostly the brothers came home with vegetables and fruits and rabbits and sometimes a wild boar for the tsarevna to turn into delicious meals for them all. She often thought of her beloved Nikolai, for she was sure he would try to find her, but then she remembered her terrible step-mother and so resigned herself to her new life.

And what of the tsarina? Everyone was still preoccupied with the loss of the tsarevna; no word had come from Nikolai, and the tsar was plunged into gloom at the loss of his beloved daughter. The tsarina hadn't looked in the mirror for a very long while, so sure was she that her beauty was the most outstanding. But one afternoon she was bored and so she smirked at the mirror and asked it, "How beautiful am I?"

The mirror replied, "Your beauty is astounding, my lady…"

The tsarina smirked some more, but the mirror continued, "but lovelier by far is the tsarevna."

The tsarina flew into the most awful rage. She screamed for Chernavka and boxed her ears until the poor girl was seeing stars. "You deceitful girl! How could you betray me so? Tell me where the tsarevna is hiding at once!" And, bit by bit, she wormed out of Chernavka that the tsarevna had been alive and well when she left her in the forest and in all probability had not been eaten by wolves. The tsarina realized that she would need to seek out the tsarevna herself, and so she flung Chernavka out of her room and began to make some terrible plans.

Some days later, the tsarevna was sitting sewing a huge button onto a huge shirt when the little dog, who had been lying peacefully at her feet, erupted into a terrible frenzy of barking. The tsarevna looked out of the huge window, and there, coming through the clearing, was an old beggar woman dressed all in black. The tsarevna fetched a hunk of bread to give to the old woman and opened the huge door. The little dog hurtled out and snarled and growled at the old woman.

"I am so sorry, I don't know what has possessed him," apologized the tsarevna. "I have some bread for you, can you catch it if I throw it over his head?"

"Bless you," muttered the old woman. "You are very kind, perhaps you would accept this apple as a thank you for your generosity?" and she threw the apple into the tsarevna's outstretched hands, then scuttled away back into the forest.

The little dog whined and tried to push the apple out of the tsarevna's hands, but she just laughed at him and took a great bite out of it. In an instant she fell to the ground, and lay quite still, no longer breathing. When the seven giants came back home later, they found their friend stretched out on the floor, lifeless, the little dog howling by her side. They tried everything they could think of to revive the tsarevna, but all to no avail.

"This is the evil tsarina's doing," said one. The others nodded, for who else would want to harm the gentle tsarevna? The giants kept watch over the tsarevna through the night, and then the next day discussed how to bury her. She looked as if she were only asleep and as beautiful as when she was alive,

and they were very reluctant to place her in a dark coffin. So they made her a special casket of crystal and laid her in that, placing it close by the house near a swiftly flowing river with flower-strewn banks that the tsarevna had often walked along. They took turns in watching over the coffin so that the tsarevna was never alone, and a great sadness descended over the huge house in the forest clearing.

Meanwhile, back at the palace, the tsarina glared at her mirror.

"Your beauty is astounding, my lady. There is no one on earth who can compare with you," said the mirror.

And the tsarina smiled a terrible smile.

Now, I hope you haven't forgotten poor Nikolai? He had searched the land for his tsarevna, over mountains and through valleys, under rivers and across forests, but not a trace had he found. He asked every wise old babushka that he met, every rusalka swimming in the rivers, every wolf and even every fierce brown bear he stood before, trembling in his boots, but no one knew where she was. He asked the sun to shine in every dark corner, but she did not know where the tsarevna was. He asked the secret moon to look behind the clouds but the moon had not seen her either. The day came when he thought he could look no longer for he was heartsore and utterly weary.

As he sat on the grass, his head cradled in his hands, a little bird chirruped in his ear, "One more step, brave Nikolai. I know where your tsarevna lies. She is in a special casket of crystal, close to a huge house near a swiftly flowing river with flower-strewn banks and she is guarded by a loving giant." When Nikolai looked up, the little bird cocked his head as if to say, "Follow me," and so he did.

He scrambled to his feet and where the bird flew, Nikolai went. Days passed and neither the bird nor Nikolai paused in their journey. But then, finally, the brave little bird led Nikolai right up to the giant who was guarding the crystal coffin. When he saw the tsarevna lying there, Nikolai caught his breath in wonder. "She looks as if she is merely sleeping!" he cried to the giant, and he laid his hand tenderly on the crystal coffin.

There was a great crack, and the coffin splintered into a million starry pieces. The tsarevna opened her eyes, and looked about her in complete wonderment. There, in front of her, stood her beloved Nikolai, and then all the giants came running up for they had heard the coffin shattering. The little bird called to all the other birds in the forest and they all raised their voices in one huge song of joy. The news spread like wildfire, "The tsarevna is alive!"

A very happy party made its way back to the palace. The giants were singing at the top of their voices, but Nikolai and the tsarevna just looked at each other in total silence, blissfully happy but unable to believe that they were really reunited once again.

Inside the palace, the tsarina was braiding her hair before the mirror. It suddenly spoke of its own volition, a thing that had never happened before. "O, wicked lady, here comes the tsarevna, and her beauty is astounding, my lady. There is no one on earth who can compare with her."

The tsarina grew white as the driven snow and then smashed her hand against the mirror in her towering rage. The mirror flew into tiny pieces, showering the tsarina in a glassy dust that snuffed out her breath. So that was the end of her!

Nikolai and the tsarevna were married the very next day, with the giant brothers forming a guard of honor and the little dog and the little bird perched on their broad shoulders. The tsar was overjoyed not only to have his dear daughter back again, but to have the strong young Nikolai by his side as well. And they really did all live happily ever after.

Sources of the Stories

Giants exist in the folklore of almost every culture. In many of the oldest myths and legends, giants are recorded as being the first race of people to exist on earth after the gods, and as usually being in conflict with the gods. According to Greek legend, the giants were sons of the earth, hence their name, which is derived from *Ge Genis* meaning "children of the earth". With the help of the human Heracles (Hercules in Roman mythology) they battled with Zeus. Heracles established the archetypal characteristics of giants in his struggles to complete the twelve labours: physical strength, endurance, enormous appetites and good humour.

In many myths and legends, giants were portrayed as being exceptionally stupid and brutish but of great might, and capable of huge feats of strength. These mighty titans were often capable of defeat by frail but resourceful and cunning heroes—and sometimes even heroines! In many legends, giants have human form, but in the Native American and some African traditions, an animal or huge bird is common. Tezcatlipoca, brother of Quetzalcoatl, devoured the entire Aztec race of giants by turning himself into an immense jaguar.

In fairy tales, giants are more likely to be bumbling but benign creatures, almost the personification of adults from a child's-eye view. Indeed, the extremes of their behaviour, from kindness to unpleasantness of varying degrees, is probably a projection of the child's view of a parent, both as the provider and the disciplinarian. It is interesting to consider that in some academic thought, the giant is seen as representing the father figure, while the witch represents the mother!

The collection here comes from a wide variety of cultures, some with clear roots and lines of descent, others with more obscure origins, but with all the expected traditional elements and ingredients, as well as a few surprises.

Mighty Mountain Unexpectedly perhaps, this story comes from *Evige Bjerg og de tre staerke kvinder* written by Irene Hedlund, and originally translated into English by Judith Elkin, a Danish version of a traditional Japanese tale.